BANK ON IT-
A WHITE COLLAR
CRIME NOVELLA

BRANDON Q. HEPBURN

PROLOGUE

My image is my money. It's how I eat. You ever heard of the saying "Perception is Reality"? Meaning, whatever a person perceives or believes, whether real or imagined, is their reality. Well, those are words that I live by; the reason I have it tattooed across my back. Because, in my world, nothing is more important than someone's, especially a woman's, view of me. Appearance is everything. You see, where dope boys get super fly in the most expensive gear and jewelry, and push the hottest whips for pleasure, fun, or just for the sport of it, for me, it's just business, a necessity.

It's why I'm up right now at 7:30 a.m. slippin' on a gray custom-fitted, short-sleeve, button-up, linen pants set, with the gray ostrich sling backs to match. Why I have on a polished, chrome and gray-faced Cartier watch. Also why I'm shining all twelve of my gold teeth (permanent) and brushing my dogs. I'm starting my daily hunt. Each day, my goal is to find and holla (court) at least five women. Then, I have to seduce 'em. But I don't want their love or even the pussy, unless necessary. I only want one thing; and that's their bank account.

The name's Chill. Here's a few tokens. Come and play in my game room for awhile.

Here's my story . . .

CHAPTER 1

"Listen, sweetie, just do exactly as I'm telling you and everything will be ok," I told Rita. Rita was a recent client that I picked up this past Saturday. I met Rita at the USA Flea market on 79th Street in Liberty City. That's where I go for my "down for whatever chicks." Most guys wouldn't give her a second, let alone a first, look, d. ue to the fact she was pushing a BMW (body made wrong). She's the same size all the way around. She don't walk; she roll. Her complexion is "burple", that's black and purple, and she looks like a pit-bull in the face. But money ain't gotta be pretty; it just gotta spend.

I saw her use the ATM machine to get some money. So I went into "attack mode." I was fitted in baby blue, velour Echo pants, with a baby blue, navy blue, and white- striped, velour Echo polo shirt, and navy blue leather Havana Joe bucks. To top things off, I had on a dope boy Cuban link with the St. Lazarus medallion and the Cuban link bracelet to match. I approached, of all places, at the food and pretzel stand. Imagine that.

I was all charm as I said, "How you doing, sweetie? I'm TQ." I held my hand out and held her stare.

"Fine, and you? My name is Rita," she replied, as she took my hand.

"Rita, it's been raining all day. But I guess that didn't stop the sun from shining."

She was all teeth and dimples. It took one day to get Rita's bank account, just on word play. She worked at McDonald's. She lived in the Pork-n-Beans (a project in Liberty City). She drove a Geo Prism. Analysis: She could use a

1

l'il extra cheese (money),. so I convinced her that I could do just that. : that leads us to where we at right now. Checks cleared and money waiting to be picked up.

"Are you sure, Ty'Quan? I'm nervous," questioned Rita.

Ty'Quan, TQ for short, is my alias when I'm in my hometown, Miami, doing business. I don't ever use my real name or my nickname(it still ties back to me, when I'm courting a potential business prospect) for safety reasons. Simply put, I don't want anyone telling on me. Matter of fact, when I have a female in the whip that I know I'm trying to seduce, I don't keep my registration, anything pertaining to my car ownership, or anything with names in the glove compartment. I hide them. Past experience dictates this, and I learn from all experiences. So, the name depends on the city; name;. in Houston I'm Mike;. In Atlanta I'm Maurice. At the crib, Miami, to those who haven't grown up with me, know me from school, or da streets, I'm TQ.

I know you're probably wondering how I can get away with that if it's my hometown, but Miami ain't no little place. I use that to my advantage. I mean, I'm street raised and book smart, so I straddle the fence when it comes to people I associate with. I consider myself twice as smart as most:. I mean can a geek thug it? Rarely. Can a street nigga get down in white America? Rarely. I do both. A gangsta and a gentleman; a hustler and a businessman.

I insisted, "I wouldn't steer you wrong, sweetie. Just remember that this is your money you're going in to get. So act like it. You can't get into any trouble for going to withdraw your own money. Look, what's bad for you is bad for me. I won't let anything happen to you, so calm down, l'il one, you're in great hands - better than Allstate."

Rita smiled, then exhaled, "Ok, TQ, tell me what to do."

My, business partner, Jap, and Rita, were at First Union Bank on Pines Boulevard in Broward county, parked not too close to the entrance, but close enough to keep an eye on the entrance doors. We were in a rented, beige 2001 Buick Park Avenue. Not too flashy, but stylish – mostly driven by older people. We always put tints on the rentals to serve our purpose of being incognito.

I turned around in the passenger seat to coach Rita. It was game time.

"All right, peep, game. Go inside just like a regular customer, cause that's what you are. Grab a withdrawal slip and fill it out for $4375.18. Remember, that – $4375.18! Jump in line; that's it. We'll be right out here waiting on you. You feel me?" I explained.

Rita replied, "Yeah, I got you. They aren't gonna ask me any questions about where the money comes from, are they?"

"Nah, it ain't their business to question you unless they see something wrong with the account. There's nothing wrong. My inside connect already gave me the ok." I shot her the fugazi (lie) about a nonexistent inside connect.

Jap added, "So go ahead and let's get this money so you can go buy them outfits you were talking bout earlier, ya dig?"

With that, she jumped out and strode to the entrance to the bank. Judging by her body language, she would be ok. If worse came to worse, we'd leave her ass right there. Rule #1: self-preservation.

"Fool, I gotta shit," mumbled Jap.

"Yeah, cause you a shitty-ass nigga," I replied and laughed.

Jap smiled and retorted, "Fuck you, nigga. That makes two of us. So stop flauging (camouflaging - lying)."

I smiled cause I knew he was right. The "shits" was part of the game. No matter how long I've been doing this, they'll always be a part of it. It comes from the suspense and uncertainty in the air. The hope that all goes well, but the thought that it won't.

"It's thirteen cars in the parking lot, fool. Counting employees' cars, she should be no more than ten minutes; fifteen at the most. She's been in there for five already." Jap observed as he scanned the parking lot.

"I saw three people go in while you were persuading Rita, so I figure that's at least three people in front of her since they haven't come out yet," stated Jap, still watching the door.

"Yeah, I got it on the clock. We still have to swerve by the crib and grab the other work (checks) to drop (deposit), after we take her home," I said.

"Well, we'll just snatch the other five dollars ($500) out of the ATM after we drop," Jap looked at me while waiting for my response.

See, our game is tried and true. We find people with jobs and tell them we'll give them $50 or $100 for a copy of their check. If they ask why do we need a copy of their check, we simply tell whoever it is that Jap or I is trying to get an apartment and the landlord wants to see proof of a job, which we don't have.

We then take that copy and remake it on the computer, putting our account holder's name on the checks and switching all the check numbers. We deposit the checks and wait for them to clear, which is usually overnight, although there are numerous factors that determine the hold on a check. We don't ever drop more than five stacks (grand) worth of checks into the account in one day. That'll red flag the account. So we typically drop three checks of sixteen hundred and change at three different banks to put us under five stacks. This process get repeated for three days for a grand total of just under fifteen stacks. Pay the accountee one stack, and it's around fourteen stacks left for Jap and I. After three days, the "bad checks" are returned to the bank, and the account is frozen; then put in the negative. Simple, right? Wrong.

It's a lot that goes into this; a lot of trial and error. Different banks, different systems – some faster, some slower. Account maintenance also matters, as well length of account history. But most importantly, the checks have to be made with the proper ink. If the checks don't scan in a bank's check reader, you're gonna be in a pretty sticky situation. But all these things can be controlled. What can't be controlled, are the whims of a teller.

"Fool, she coming out," exclaimed Jap.

"Her body language looks like everything is straight," I observed.

"Yeah, she grinning and cheesing like she hit the lottery," chuckled Jap.

I could tell he was relieved; so was I. But we still had work to do, so celebrations had to wait. Rita got in the back seat and everyone was quiet until Jap exited the bank parking lot.

"Everything good?" I asked Rita, although I already knew the answer.

"Yeah, the teller was real nice. A young black girl, asking me about my pigtails. Here you go," she excitedly passed me the chips (money). I counted it, gave her five dollars ($500). She'd get the rest on the third day, if it made it that far. Give her something to look forward to, keep her motivated. I put the rest in my pocket. Jap and I handle business alone.

"Thank you, TQ," Rita stated happily.

Shit, fifteen minutes worth of work for $500. I'd be happy too if I didn't know the repercussions – but I do. In most cases, the bank puts your account in the negative for all the money you fraudulently withdrew. That means you owe them. If you don't pay, it goes on your credit.

Which is why i go to the hood for females a lot, because majority of the time, their credit is already fucked up. But in some cases, just like now, they still get mad. That happens when I tell them my aunt works in whatever bank I find out their at and that she's going to wire some money into their, the accountee's, account by manipulating the bank's computer system. Then she's going to clear out the transaction.

This is what I told Rita. She's gonna be pissed when she finds out we dropped some bogus ass checks in her account. But, oh, well, by that time, I'll be gone in the wind. I don't feel bad cause you can't make a honest muhfucha commit crimes. All you need is dirt the size of a mustard seed to be dirty.

"No problem, sweetie. You earned that. Don't spend all your chips on B.S. – I. know you don't have any kids, but pay a bill or two, ya dig?" I told Rita.

"I feel you. Are you gonna holla (call) at me later?" asked Rita.

"Fo sho. I have to let you know what time I'm coming in da morning. So make sure you're on point. Reliability is a beautiful characteristic," I stated.

"One thing I want you to know, TQ, is that you can always count on me. I am very loyal and I keep it gangsta, boo. Remember that."

"I hear you," I replied unenthusiastically.

Because I done heard it all before. Shit, some of it I made up. We pulled up in front of Rita's crib and let her out. On some friend-type shit, Rita ain't a bad person to vibe (chill) with. But friends turn into enemies. So the fewer the better. Jap and I made off to finish our jobs.

CHAPTER 2

Everything went as planned with Rita and her account. It lasted three days, and Jap and I made off with a little under seven stacks a piece – all profit. That's the difference between the "B" and the "D" game. I don't have to hustle back up my re-up before I see any profit. It's all profit! Every time I bust an account, I think about how this bank shit changed my life.

Jap and I first met in the sixth grade. Since then, he's been my ace. He's who told me how to find the hole when I lost my virginity at fourteen. He lost his at eleven. Jap and his family are Haitian. It took a while for them to accept me. But ever since, they've treated me like one of their own. When we got to high school, we attended different schools. He went to Hialeah Miami Lakes High, and I went to Norland in Carol City. But we were still tighter than virgin pussy.

Around 10th grade, I started hangin' in my neighborhood projects, Cloverleaf. They were located down the street from my house and school. When we skipped school, that's where we went. Soon, I found myself spending more time in the Leaf than in school. I went from hangin' to slangin' in no time. By the age of fourteen, I was serving base, butta, and sense (rocks, coke, and weed). Jap wasn't a D-boy. He was always infatuated with some female, plus he was working at Papa John's. But he had the whip, and I had the chips. I eventually got kicked out of school and hustled full time. Jap skipped himself outta school, too. Birds of a feather...

Sometime in '96, when I was seventeen, one of Jap's older cousins, Rouseau, tried to put down (dope) in the Leaf. Rou was in his early thirties and was a cool nigga who was getting money. But my fools wasn't even with it. You ain't from around here, ain't no serving – period. I tried to warn him, something I normally wouldn't do, cause he was Jap's cousin. He wouldn't listen, so my homeboys tried to slump (murder) him.

He had a l'il female's apartment he was grindin' out of. One night, my homeboys decided it was time to teach Rou the repercussions of disrespecting the game. Three weeks prior to this, I got roped off (locked up) on a sales charge. It just so happened, that on that particular night they were to rob him, I got released. At the crib, everybody knew twenty-one days and you out. The good ole days! I called Brianna, a l'il female that the boys be knockin' off (fuckin) in the hood. She also doubled as a "hood assistant." I was super happy to see her raggedy-ass Chevy Cavalier put at DCJ (Dade County Jail). I got in.

"What up, l'il momma?" I asked.

"Boy, where you been?" she asked. Stupid ass question.

"I been on the moon. Where it look like I been?"

"You know what I mean, Chill. How you doing?" she replied, and pushed me.

"I'm good. Happy to be out that shit. What's going on in the hood?"

"Same ol' shit, different day. Dem crackas been real hot lately. DT (detectives) been coming through a lot, ever since Flip beat his girl ass last week. He broke her arm and swoll up dat girl face. His fuck ass. Somebody need to whoop his ass!"

"So what, she press charges?"

"Damn right. You shoulda seen dat girl face. She look like she got stung by a thousand bumblebees. I woulda cut his ass up, he woulda put his hands on me," she said, more with her neck than her mouth.

"Girl, you ain't gonna knock a fly off a birthday cake. So stop flaugin (pretending)."

"Whateva, let a nigga try." She reached over, grabbed my dick, and playfully rubbed it.

"Damn, I know you gonna give a bitch some of dat good dick tonight. You know you backed up. I had dis pussy' waitin on you," she looked at me in, what was supposed to be, a seductive manner.

"Oh, yeah, how long she been waiting for me? A couple hours," I replied sarcastically.

She laughed and said, "Fuck you, Chill. You know you want dis good pussy. Oh, yeah, what's up wit' yo boy?"

"Who?"

"Jap cousin, Roule, Rodney – whateva his name is," she replied.

"Rouseau? What about him?"

"You betta tell him to get his ass from round there. Tech and 'em talkin bout dey gone deal wit' him. You know how you and yo' friends is."

"Yeah, when you heard dis?" I questioned.

"'Bout two nights ago."

"Silly-ass nigga shoulda been got missin from round there. I'll check it out when we get 'round da way."

"Do dat. Cause he kind of cute. Dat be a waste of dick if they do something to him," she smiled.

I looked at her, "You forever thinkin' wit' ya clit, huh?"

"Betta than not thinkin' at all," she laughed.

"Girl, you stupid."

When we got to da Leaf, I told her to swing me by the trap. But when we got there, it was lookin' like a ghost town on this side. Damn – 10:00 p.m. on a Saturday! Dem crackas must be hot.

"Swing me by da 505 building."

Cloverleaf consisted of ten two-story apartment buildings.

The 505 building was where Rouseau stayed. When we pulled up, I got out, looked around, and took in da scenery. It was a cool February night. People outside were smoking, drinking, playing stereos – and there were even some kids still outside. I walked through the cut to Rou's first floor apartment and knocked on the door. No one answered after a couple minutes, and I couldn't hear anything coming from inside. As I turned to leave, that's when the door cracked open slightly.

I looked in the crack so Rou could see it was me. The door opened halfway, and I saw a familiar silhouette. Skinny Man was holding some fire (gun) with a savage looking facial expression.

I knew what time it was.

I eased into the apartment.

"Y'all niggas loose," I exclaimed frustratedly, as I looked around.

I saw Tech standing in the bedroom doorway, watching me and Doc standing in the kitchen looking through the wall server. I'm thinking, "Where's Rou and Tabitha?"

"Fool, we know dis Jap people. But, my nigga, we gave this fuck-boy plenty time to clear it from round here. But he wanna try da hood like we pussy!," Skinny Man stated passionately.

"Dat nigga think cause we young niggas we won't do his ass in," Tech spit out angrily.

"Chill, Chill, my nigga, tell your homeboys let me go dawg. I'll pack it up (leave)," I heard Rou's voice yell nervously from the kitchen.

Thud. Grunt. I knew that sound anywhere. Doc slapped Rou with the pistol.

"Fuck nigga, no talking. You shoulda left when we told yo hoe ass to leave!," Doc spit out venomously.

I walked to the kitchen entrance and saw Rou tied to a chair with phone cords.

"Chill – please dawg. I'll drop you a bet. They can keep everything found and I'll throw you some mo' bread, Chill."

Smack. Smack. Grunt. Doc front and backhand slapped him.

"Fuck nigga, didn't I say shut up?" Doc yelled.

"Hold up, D," I said.

"Man, fuck dis nigga, Chill. You still takin' up for dis nigga. You switchin' out on da hood, my nigga?" Tech questioned angrily, as he walked up behind me.

I turned around and faced him, "Hold up, fool. Chill out, fool. Don't take you anger out on me."

"I'm sayin', nigga, CLB. This our shit, my nigga; this our hood!" Tech yelled.

"Yeah, nigga, I feel you. I ain't never said I don't feel y'all boys. Shit, if it was anyone else, I'd a run off in here wit' y'all niggas. But dis Jap peoples. We can't kill dis nigga, my nigga," I explained.

Skinny Man walked from the living room and asked, "So what we supposed to do? Let dis nigga go so he can try and get back? My nigga, you know how we roll. No loose ends, fool. Remember?"

"Alright. Peep da play. Hold up. Hold up. Hold up. Hold up. Where da fuck Tab at?" I asked suddenly.

Thinking 'bout this nigga, Rou, I had forgotten all about Tab. D was still standing in da kitchen behind me next to Rou. I was in the kitchen entrance, facing the hall leading to the living room one way and the bedroom the other. Tech was standing next to me on my left side, facing Skinny Man and the living room, and Skinny was on my right, facing Tech and the bedroom.

"We got dat hoe right in here," Tech answered, and reached to the hallway closet door. On the wall opposite the kitchen entrance, when he opened it, I saw Tab on her back, with her legs and hands in the air, tied together with, shit, look like some type of electrical cords. She was sweating and her eyes were wide with fear. Her mouth was gagged and taped.

I stepped forward and shut the door.

"Alright, peep game. What all y'all came up on?" I asked.

Skinny walked to the living room couch and came back with a shopping bag. We all stepped into the kitchen and emptied the contents on the counter. I saw two gallon-size ziplocks, one filled with a bunch of dimes and the other with twenties – all crack. Had to be about five stacks worth of dimes, probably double in twenties. There were also two separate stacks of cash, banded off. Another zip filled with soft white, look like 'bout three or four zincs (ounces).

"Y'all know we can't slump dis nigga," I stated.

"Shit, why not?" Skinny and Doc asked at the same time.

"If we do, my nigga, we gone have to lean Tab ass too. Even if we leave some twenties and a l'il coke to make it look drug related, this shit will be hot for a minute. That's two bodies. Even though dem crackas don't care. They gotta act like it, for that. Remember, it's still square's lives around here and dem crackas gotta look like they doing something. We ain't gone be able to get no money for a l'il minute. Jumpout (task) gone be in anybody ass that post up in da cut. Matter of fact, how y'all got in here?"

"We had that hoe Tab come and knock on da door. We knew da nigga knew we at his ass. So he looked out da peep and saw it was her. When dat nigga opened it to let her in, we let her get halfway in and kicked da door in, my nigga. Fuck, nigga had fire but he dropped it when da door hit him, and he hit da wall," Skinny answered.

Tab was a white lady, a baser (crack addict) who was also a nurse. Everybody knew when she came through, she spending big.

"Man, dat's a witness right there. We gone have to kill her too if we kill him. Look, my nigga, we need to just take da sac and da chips and hit it. On da real, G shit," I explained.

"Yeah, y'all can have dat shit. I don't want it, my nigga. I won't come through – period. Please, just let me go," Rou pleaded.

Bam.

Tech kicked him in the chest and knocked the chair over backwards.

"Pussy nigga, did we ask you?" Tech questioned malevolently.

"Chill, right y'all. I'd rather deal wit' da streets and retaliation than deal wit' dem crackas. We can handle dat creep ass nigga on da floor, but dem crackas is another story," Skinny agreed.

"So put that shit back in da bag. Let's clear it, my nigga."

We put da loot in da bag and made to leave.

Tech said, "Hold up. I'm takin' dis nigga yopper (AK). Skinny, you got dat Gloc he had, right?"

"Fo' sho," Skinny replied.

"What? Y'all wanna untie 'em too?" D asked.

"Nah," I replied. "They'll find a way to get free. As happy as they are that they living."

I opened the closet door and told Tab, "Fa ya own good don't bring dem crackas in dis. Cause I promise, we'll find you 'fo dey find us, ya feel me?"

She nodded her head and whimpered.

We walked to the door.

"Bet dat up, Chill," Rou cried out.

I didn't look back. I didn't respond.

I didn't really save him for him. I did it out of respect for Jap. That's my nigga.

"Nah, let's go dis way. I got dat hoe Brianna waiting. Dat's who picked me up from da jailhouse," I told 'em.

"Yeah, a nigga ready to fuck somethin' anyway. I thought you got out Monday," stated Tech.

"Dats why you need to finish school, my nigga," I said as we jumped in Brianna's hooptie. "Monday would've been twenty-three days, not twenty-one."

The fellas laughed as the tension eased.

"Fuck you, nigga," Tech said playfully.

Doc called out, "CLB."

"Fo' life," we all cried out together.

———

Later that year, me and the rest of CLB (Cloverleaf Boys) got into a war with a rival gang and bodies started droppin'. I went on da run. I hid out on Biscayne Boulevard, a street that's lined with motels on both sides. They cater to pimps, pushers, tricks, basers, prostitutes, and any other form low life. I crashed at different motels: Vegabond, Stardust, Davis, Economy Inn, and more. It's easy to get lost on the 'Cayne' cause it's a world unto itself.

I still had to eat, so I had Jap holla at Rou, and I began copping (buying) from him. He'd bring whatever I needed to me. I didn't have to go nowhere, and that was a luxury I needed. I stayed on my grind, but shit was taking its toll on me. The crackas had already roped off five of my niggas. It was only a few of us left. I knew they were on my trail.

One day, early morning, Jap and Rou came and hollered at me. They told me to take a ride with them. I must admit, it felt good to get out. Being cooped up for the last two months, having not seen family or friends. Rou had a beige Jeep Wagoneer with wood paneling around the doors and 16-inch chrome KMCs and chunky tires.

Jap looked back at me. I could see some type of joy in his eyes.

"What's up, fool?" I asked them curiously.

We were turning out of the Stardust parking lot, headed down Biscayne. The day was sunny and warm.

Rou replied, "I was telling Jap that I want y'all to spend the day with me. I want to show y'all some new things. I'm gonna put y'all up on game, ya feel me?"

Watching Rou, and knowing how he vibed, I knew it was about cheddar. Rou had on a fourteen carat dopeboy Cuban link chain that was heavy and thick. I knew it cost at least six stacks cause I priced them. He had a four link Cuban link bracelet with a nameplate in the middle – his name spelled in diamonds. Plus, he had diamonds on every finger except his thumbs. The nigga was fresh in a blue and white Tommy pullover short set. Those were my Dickie days – the only thing I wore, seven days a week. Seeing how fly dat nigga was, I was ready and listening.

Rou explained, "It's a whole 'nother world out there, Chill," he said to me, calling me by the name I earned by "chillin" in nigga's yards, waiting for them to come home. "Everything isn't about dope, l'il fool. It's some things out here that are a lot safer and will make you just as much, or even more money, but you gotta expand your mind. Now, see, I respect you're gangsta. But that's just it; being gangsta is only one side of things. The other is being smart. What do you know about credit cards and check scams?"

"Oh, dat's what dem l'il females and sissys be on," responded Jap.

"Yeah, dat's how da twins eat," I cut in, speaking of me and Jap's homegirls out the hood that be on that boosting shit and scheming credit cards. They stole us a bunch of 'fits(outfits) over the years.

"See, that's just it. It's not just for females and sissys, as y'all say. It's for everbody. Do you know the difference between blue-collar and white-collar crime? Serving dope is blue-collar. Checks are white-collar," Rou said.

"Man, it's all crime – shit!" exclaimed Jap.

"Shut up, dumb nigga, and listen," Rou shot at Jap.

"A crime isn't just a crime. Why do you think you see Hispanic and black people in jail the most? What, you don't think crackas do crimes? Nah, it's because they do smart crimes. White-collar crime carries little or no time.

Think about it. If you go to the Fed for dope, unless you telling, they handing out dinosaur years. But if you go for checks, banks, insurance fraud, embezzlement…"

"What's embezzlement?" questioned Jap.

Rou responded, "Stealing or taking money or property out of a business by using fraud. You know, like how them crackas be CEOs or presidents of companies and swindle money out the company by lying about the profits or using phony income tax schemes. Peep game, if you go to the Fed for any one of those things, nine times out of ten, you'd be home in five years or less. You might just get restitution and probation."

"So, you saying if I sold a million dollars worth of dope, them crackas a hide my ass forever, but if I embezzle a million dollars, I'll be home in five or less. Why?" I asked, not certain if I was going for this shit he was spitting at us.

"Simple. Because them crackas would rather have you scammin' paper and computers, which is ultimately insured, than slingin' guns and dope, killing up people, being a menace to society. The lesser of the two evils. While they're eating shrimp and playing golf, we're in Marion fighting for our lives. White-collar crime has been going on since the beginning of time. But that's just it; majority were white people doing them. Most blacks didn't have the resources, connects, or the knowledge. But some of us do now."

"And you finna let us in your game?" I asked.

I must admit, the shit sounded good and I was hoping like hell he was for real. But I also know there's a catch to everything. Ain't nobody passing on game for free.

I asked, "Why?"

"Chill, you looked out for me a while back, so I'm gonna clean my face (pay you back)," he responded, speaking on the time I stopped him from getting killed.

"You saved my life, so I'm gonna save yours. And, Jap, you're my l'il cousin. I'm just tired of seeing you with that tight ass Papa John outfit. You look like a male stripper."

We all laughed.

"So y'all sit back and observe," Rou stated, as we got on the ramp for the I-95 North.

"Where we headed?" Jap asked.

"Fort Lauderdale," replied Rou, as he looked at Jap and then, in the rearview, at me.

"We have a few deposits to make," he stated, as he turned up 2 Pac's "Picture Me Rollin" and smashed the gas on the I. That's how it all began.

But it wasn't all peaches and cream. For one, not long after I learned the game in '96, I finally got roped off by the nuts(police) in June of '97. I was sick. Jap, Rou, and I had just bought a four-bedroom house in upscale North Miami Beach, right before my birthday in December of '96. Jap and me were young niggas, so we weren't on luxury wheels.

We copped 1973 Chevy Impalas (Donks). Mine was money-green, candy painted, with gold flakes. I had money-green original vinyl interior with matching carpet, four Pioneer twelve-inch tube speakers in the trunk, with Pioneer mids and highs, and a Pioneer flipout radio with a twelve-disk Pioneer CD changer. It was running a 454 up under the hood with Flow Masters out the back, sitting on eighteen-inch triple gold Daytons. Jap's was similar, but his was painted candy-apple red with matching interior.

Things were cool between us when I left the streets, except Rou was shaking us on the chips from our scams. It was alright at first, 'cause game meant to be sold not told. So we were just paying the cost of the come up. I know when it's my time to pass the game I'm taxing the shit outta whoever it is. But I sat in DCJ (Dade County Jail) for twenty-four months before they dropped the MI charge. My fools kept it G code – plus, dead men don't talk.

In that time, I got my GED and took a couple of college courses – business management and finance. The whole time I was down, Jap held me down, but us and Rou fell out over cash. Jap was tired of getting whooped, and so was I. So we stopped fucking with that nigga and broke off on our own. We had acquired enough game and skills. It was time to leave the nest.

In the time I was locked up, Jap married a l'il female named L'Shay he met at the Dade County Youth fair before I got held hostage in the jailhouse. He was always soft on females.

This one here was like six years older than us and locked him down. I just hope it doesn't come back to bite him in the ass. But since I came home in '99, up until now, '01, Jap and I have been getting loot. But we don't super hang out, with him being on wifey restrictions.

I ain't gonna lie, I miss tricking with my nigga. She don't let him do shit, and he pays all the bills. I can't comprehend that shit. I always ask him, "Who wears the pants, my nigga, you or her?" He rarely steps out. So the bank accounts typically fall on me to get. But that's ok. I'm getting paid to do something I love, and that's vibing up females. But at the same time, I keep feeling there's got to be a better way to do this. But I'll find it. Patience – that's my name, ain't it?

CHAPTER 3

JAP
FRIDAY, 4:50 P.M.

We had a light week this week. Compared to some weeks, when we have two or three accounts to do. Things have been really good since Chill came home. It makes a big difference that he is single and I'm not. He can go a lot more places and meet a lot more people. Sometimes I think this marriage shit is holding me back. But every time I look at Japhier Poitier, Jr., my three-year-old son, it erases all doubt.

My father wasn't around at all. So it brings me great joy to be here for my shorty (child). Plus, I know it makes him happy to see his mother and father still together. But, yet, I sometimes can't help but envy Chill and his freedom. I respect the fact that, despite his bachelorhood, he still plays a major and active role in his son's life. Seeing that keeps my playa' fantasies fueled on low.

<RING RING>

My cell phone. I should've known it was Shay calling, just getting off work.

"Hey, baby," I answer.

"What's up? Where you at?" she questions.

"It's five o'clock. Where you think I'm at?

Picking up our son," I replied sarcastically.

She retorted in the usual Shay smart-mouth fashion.

"It's actually 4:53. So, like I asked, where you at?"

"Girl, I just pulled up to the daycare. Now if you let me off the pipe, I can go inside."

"Why you need me to get off the phone so you can go inside? What, you got something going on with one of them hoes in there?"

I looked at the phone. Stupid-ass girl. I loved her to death, but sometimes I just didn't like her ass.

I replied, heatedly, "Man, get off my phone." I pressed the end button and got out my car to go get my son.

<RING RING>

"What, girl?" I answered.

"Are y'all coming straight home?"

"I need to stop by Trap house and pick something up."

Trap had a couple of paychecks that he got from two of his girls. I'm going to pay him $200 for both.

"Come home first. I need to show you something."

"I'll be there after I pick up this shit from fool."

"Always putting me on the back burner for your friends," she responded, and hung up.

"What the fuck was she talking about?" I thought, standing on the sidewalk in front of the daycare. I don't do shit and rarely go anywhere. Man, let me get Jr. and go to the house to see what she want.

I picked up Jr. and took him to McDonald's on the way home – the whole time feeling guilty about something I probably didn't do. Do I really put my friends before her? Is all her crabbing a way of reaching out? Maybe we need a l'il vacation; some time away.

Yeah, that might be the answer. We haven't had one of those in a minute. I could show her it's all about her. This was my thought process as my son and I entered our condo. "Baby, your men are home," I called out.

We stayed in a three-bedroom condo in a gated community in exclusive Miami Lakes. We had all the amenities one could possibly want, in and out of the apartment: Rec-centers, tennis courts, workout centers, a park, Jacuzzis, in and out, and pools. For our ages, I was 23, she was 28, we were way ahead of the game.

We are blessed!

L'Shay walked out of our bedroom and met us in the living room.

"Hey, mommy baby," she said to our son. Jr. ran to his mother, and she scooped him up.

"Hey, boobie. Were you a good boy at daycare?"

"Yes," Jr. answered, while nodding his head.

"Daddy bought you some food?" she asked, eyeing his bag on the table.

"Where's mommy's food?"

Jr. shrugged his shoulders and pointed at me. She eyed me but didn't speak. I know she's playing with him. She doesn't eat fast food. She set him down in his high chair and spread out his food for him.

"Damn, hello to you, too!" I stated, annoyed.

"Yeah, umm, hmm," she managed.

"So what you gotta holla at me about?"

"It don't matter. You act like you ain't wanna come and see, so don't worry about it."

"I'm here, ain't I?"

"Yeah. Whatever. For how long?"

"Man, I'm always here, girl. So what's on your mind?"

We were standing in the living room while Jr. was eating in the dining room.

"I'm straight. I don't even want to talk about it. Don't you have some business to handle, since your homeboys are so important?"

"Baby, you my business. Don't nothin' come before you and our family."

"Hmm. I can't tell."

She walked off towards the bedroom, and I followed.

"Why you following me? Go tend to your business."

I reached out and grabbed her arm and turned her around. "Come here, baby."

"Move. Let me go, Jap. Why you wanna grab on me? Grab on your friends."

"Stop playing!" I pulled her close and hugged her. "Tell me what it is that's on your mind. Your thoughts are important to me."

"That's what your mouth says. I'm going to take a shower. If you're still here when I get out, then I might talk to you."

With that, she turned and walked to our private bath. I went to see if Jr. was finished eating and get him cleaned up. Maybe something was bothering Shay. I wondered if she was pregnant again. I need to start watching some of that Oprah shit or Lifetime so I can recognize a woman's problems.

"Come on l'il man. Let me get you cleaned up," I told Jr. as I took him outta his high chair.

"We gonna make mommy smile, right?" He shook his head yes.

"We gotta make mommy happy. You want mommy to be happy, right?"

We headed to his bedroom.

"Yes, mommy happy," he smiled.

It ain't gonna hurt for me to sit at the crib for a while and spend some time with the family. I might as well bathe my jit. By the time I finish, she'll be out the shower.

"Come on, let's take a bath, Jr."

"Yeaaa!" he yelled happily, and ran to his bathroom. He loved taking baths.

<RING RING>

<RING RING>

My cell was ringing in the living room. I ran and grabbed it. It was Trap.

"What dey do, fool?" I asked.

"You still coming to get this work, right?"

"Fo' sho. I'm at the crib, getting ready to bathe jit and I'll be outta here after that. Why? You finna head out?"

"Nah, I was just checkin' 'cause you said you was gonna be here around 5:30. But, shit, I might go gambling later . But if I go, and you ain't made it, I'll hit you up before I leave. We can meet up somewhere."

"Right, right, fo' sho. I'll holla, fool," I hung up.

It ain't shit but 6:10. I'll just lamp at the crib for a couple of hours, spend some time wit' da wife, then I'll bend one. I cut my phone off and went to bathe jit.

CHAPTER 4

L'SHAY

I know my husband is a good man. That's why sometimes I feel guilty about the things I do. But other times, I just remember that's what my mother said about my father. Until she found out he was fucking her best friend for three years out of their ten-year marriage. Plus, he had twins out of wedlock from another woman. When I think about those things, that makes me say "fuck that," I'm going to get mine first.

I'm not gonna be a damn fool and sit round and wait. So, yeah, I got a fuck buddy on the side. Ain't nothin' serious, just insurance. Don't get me wrong. I love my husband, and I love our lifestyle. But that's just it. He brings home too much money to not be fucking something. I know he is.

There is no one who can tell me different. It's my women's intuition. His best friend is a modern-day crooked-ass Romeo. I don't know though. Maybe that's just my guilty conscience talking. Maybe that's why I don't give his ass room to breathe.

Maybe I'm making excuses to cheat on him. Maybe I just don't want him to do to me what I'm doing to him. Maybe I cheat cause I like it. Maybe it's not him and it's me. What if I'm some kind of freak? What if it's just in my blood? What if, maybe, I'm just a "daddy's little girl"? Sob. Cry. Sob. Cry.

CHAPTER 5

JAP
FRIDAY, 9:30 P.M.

I just put Jr. down for bed. We watched "Shrek" together as a family. Jr. really enjoyed that. I must admit, I did too. I walked back out to the living room and sat next to Shay. Damn, it's about time for me to call up Trap.

I don't want wifey to trip, especially after the day we've had. But why should I feel like I can't move when I want to? Shit, I pay all the bills. She works for MetroDade Transit and makes damn good money, but I make it to where we don't even use any of her money. I provide everything we need and more. If I don't hustle, we can't live like this in spite of the money she makes. She just gonna have to understand I gotta move when I gotta move. The game don't wait for no one.

"Baby, I gotta go pick up dat work from Trap," I said to her as, we sat on the couch with me massaging her feet.

"Ok, baby. Umm, that feels good. Please, just ten more minutes."

"Alright. You like that, huh?" I began stroking each toe, one by one.

"Ahh, psst… Ooohh, boy. You making me horny."

"Well, let me stop cause I gotta handle business," I made to get up.

"Unn, unn, come here. I wanna tell you something," she said anxiously as she sat up, pushed me back down, and straddled me.

"You been saying that all day and I ain't hear you say nothin' yet."

"I'm going to tell you right now."

She stuck her tongue in my ear, then sucked on my earlobe. She proceeded to stroke my dick through my pants. She kissed on my neck, then my chin, then my mouth. She sucked on my bottom lip, then stuck her tongue in my mouth. We tongue wrestled.

She pulled back and took my shirt off. Her tongue teased my nipples. Damn, that feel good. She stood up in front of me and pulled her night-gown over her head. She was now standing in her birthday suit. What a sight she was.

My wife is 5'8", 160 pounds, all solid, pecan tan with a waist so small I can damn near put my two hands on each side and make my fingertips touch. Flat stomach, no stretch marks; she kept it oiled while she was pregnant. With that sexy-ass line of hair from her belly button down to her pubic hair. Her hips are wide, and the ass is fat and firm, thanks to them squats. Her face is oval-shaped with honey brown teardrop shaped yes and a wide, full mouth. Her hair was styled in a wrap to her back – all hers. Dat pussy was super plump. I wanted to taste her. I sat up to do just that. She pushed me back against the couch and dropped to her knees in front of me.

The whole time, there were no words, only eye contact. I could just feel sensuality coming off of her. She slowly unbuckled my belt and unbuttoned my pants; all the while watching me. I was rock solid 10 minutes ago, but, at this point, I was so hard I ached. That's when she took all of me in her mouth, a classic deep throat. I put my head back against the couch, closed my eyes, and moaned. I could hear the slurping noise.

"Baby, do you hear me talking now?" she asked seductively.

Did I ever! I opened my eyes and looked at her with my dick in her mouth. I responded, "Girl, you shouldn't talk with your mouth full."

She smiled and resumed work.

———

Trap had called Jap's phone at least seven or eight times. It was now after midnight. He had been gambling for the last few hours at Rou's carwash/gambling house. Yeah, it was payday. But his check was already gone. They raped him in the tonk game. He was now in bounce back mode like every nigga with a gambling problem. Only thing, he ain't have no chips to bounce back with.

"Damn, this nigga still got his phone off," said Trap to himself.

He had stepped outside to try and call Jap for the millionth time. Rou and Dave was outside smoking a joint.

"Boy, you alright? They peeled your head back on the tonk table, huh?" asked Rou.

"Hell, nah – I ain't alright. I done lost my whole check. I'm trying to call – matter of fact, I'm trying to call yo' cousin. He 'posed to have a couple dollars for me," Trap explained.

"What, he owe you some money?"

"Nah, he was finna buy something from me. Come to think of it – don't you still fuck wit dat bank shit?" Trap asked.

"I don't know. Why?" Rou asked cautiously.

"He was supposed to buy these check copies I had these females make, but da nigga phone off."

"What kind of check copies? You got them on you?" Rou asked, with a poker face to hide his interest.

"Yeah, they in da car."

"Let me check 'em out."

They walked over to Trap's vehicle. Trap went inside the car and grabbed the checks.

"Let me see what you talking about," stated Rou curiously.

"You just got these today, huh? They clean?"

"Yeah, they clean – unused. I got 'em earlier from my homegirls."

"How much was he gonna give you for these? Don't try to pimp me neither!" Rou told him knowingly.

"I wouldn't try you like dat, my nigga. He usually pays a hundred and fifty a piece."

"Yeah? Check this. I'm gonna give you two hundred a piece, my nigga. From now on, when you get these, holla at me, you feel me? You don't have to worry about me cutting my phone off and shit," Rou shot sarcastically. "I'm about my business."

"Fo' sho. Dat's a bet," Trap said excitedly and gave Rou dap.

Rou gave him four hundred dollars. "I'm gonna teach that nigga to pay homage," thought Rou.

Trap took his money and went back in the gambling house to bounce back – or not!

Rou plotted.

CHAPTER 6

CHILL
SATURDAY, 12:30 A.M.

<BUZZZZ BUZZZZ>

My cell phone was vibrating. I peeped the screen. I knew it was my fool, M1. Probably wondering what in the hell was taking so long. "What dey do, boy?" "I'm getting dressed right now, fool." I cut him off at the pass.

"Damn, ol' pretty ass nigga. What, you shavin' ya chest hairs or somethin'? My nigga, tighten up."

"Oh, you got jokes, huh? Nah, I'm walking out da door right now. I'm on da way. The club don't close to five in the morning. You wanna be in da club like a job and shit."

"Whatever, nigga. I'm waiting," he hung up.

M1 was my nigga from high school and the CLB days. He was a couple years older than me. So when I didn't have a whip, he'd be the one to take me to re-up or if I had to go anywhere, he was there. He didn't ask for gas money or nothin'. Even when I was rolling hard with Rou and Jap, he was always in the background. He still do his thing on the sac tip (dope), and I can count on him to go to war with me or for me.

I was at my bachelor pad in Miami Shores – the spot I used when I was in the vicinity. I had another crib in Broward County that was my main residence, but it was super far out the way. So I copped something inside Dade city limits. A nigga been working all week, it's time to unwind. But then again, club, females – I'm such a workaholic!

I stood in the mirror and put my deodorant on. I stopped and checked myself out to make sure everything was on point. I'm 6'3", 198 pounds. I wasn't

26

cocky, but I was defined by playing basketball in school. I had a burnt orange complexion and kept my hair cut low with sideburns and a goatee. I kept a manicure and a pedicure. Hygiene is super important.

I was on point.

I slipped on my black silk Gucci pants and shirt, with the G buttons. I slipped on black Gucci loafers over black Gucci socks. Everything was subtle and understated. No G's all over my fit. I topped it off with a Gucci watch with a black leather band, gold-rimmed black face, accented with Gucci darkboys with gold rims and an all-black Gucci bucket hat with a green and red strap around the border; the only true identifier that my ensemble was pure Gucci. I was ready to roll.

I jumped in my whip. Out of all my cars, I had a '73 Chevy Impala convertible, a '65 Chevy Impala SS, a 2000 Buick Park Avenue and the one I'm in now; the one that the high-end women loved. I know most people love Benz's and Beemers, but I chose an all-black Audi A8. It competes with the BMW 750 or Benz 600 – same league, same German engineering.

Mine has black leather guts and the highest quality technology that's out. I've smartly spent well over a hundred thou on this whip, and it's helped me to make a whole lot more – appearance and image.

When we pulled into the parking lot at Club Bermuda's, it was ridiculous. The line for the front entrance was swollen. The line leading upstairs for VIP was super congested with women. That was ok cause there was enough of me to go around. We whipped up by the entrance, jumped out, and let the valets grab the car.

You could just feel all the eyes watching the contrast we created. We were fresh. My dawg had on a long-sleeved, button-down, snow-white, tailored linen two-piece with all-white Bally loafers and a white Kangol. He had on a Cuban link so thick you could tie up a pit bull with it and twenty permanent gold teeth to match. To top it off, he had on a diamond pinkie ring that looked like he won it in the Super Bowl and a diamond frosted Michael Kors time-piece with the white leather band.

We don't do lines. So we headed over to the VIP stairs and went right to the front. I held my credit card in the air, signaling we were buying bottles. They take your debit or credit card so you can't run off while the hostess leads you to your table. He lifted the velvet rope and signaled the hostess. She came and escorted us to the VIP area and our table.

I looked downstairs at the crowd before we went in, just to photograph some of my intended targets. But when I saw the stares, I knew I didn't have to make a move, cause the women would be at us tonight.

We got situated at our VIP table and ordered four fifths of Remi Martin XO at fifteen hundred dollars per bottle and an extra snifter. Once they brought our drinks, we filled up the extra snifter with the cognac, put it in the middle of our table, and set it on fire. We let the blue flame burn. We sat back and observed our surroundings. What beautiful surroundings they were.

The inside of the club has three bars downstairs and one for the VIP. The VIP also had three pool tables. There were palm plants scattered throughout, giving the club an islandesque feel. Plus, you can order food, like chicken fingers, mozzarella sticks, and such. And the women were beautiful and plenty! I leaned back on the leather couch. It was on and poppin'.

"So, I see you dopeboys still gettin a l'il paper, huh?" I teased M1.

"Yeah, you bank niggas could learn something from us." Four bad bitches walked by staring, thick to death.

I called out, "Damn ladies, my momma always told me, you see something you want, go for it.'"

They stopped.

I already knew which one I wanted. She was red- boned and chunky with a Baby Phat fit that accentuated every curve of her body. I stood up with my drink and stood directly in front of her and her friends. I reached for her hand and lifted it to my lips.

"How you beautiful ladies doing?" I asked. I looked each one in the eye. If used right, compliments lowered a woman's defenses.

"We're ok. By the looks of things, you and your friend are doing well, too," she responded.

"Yeah, y'all up here burning liquor and stuff. Must be nice," another one said.

She sweating hard. She'll probably fuck a nigga in the bathroom right now.

"I'm Ty'Quan. That's my cousin M1, and we'd be doing even finer if you ladies would join us for a drink," I said smoothly.

By this time, I had spotted the one in the group who'd be rushing them to hurry up if she didn't get no play.

I looked her dead in the eye.

"We know y'all tryin' to do y'all thing. So we won't hold y'all long. Besides worse come to worse, y'all get free drinks out the deal," I joked.

"Boy, you silly," the one I wanted said.

"And you sexy. So now that we gave each other pet names, how 'bout you give me your real name?"

"Umm," one of her homegirls said.

"I'm Amelia. That's my sister, Erica. And those are our homegirls, Ciera and Denise," explained Amelia.

I shook all of their hands, then went back to Amelia.

"Come sit down. Let's have a drink."

As soon as everyone sat down, the waitress, whose name I found out to be Tiffany, came over.

"Y'all need something else?" Tiff asked.

M1 responded, "Tiff, can you bring these ladies whatever they want?"

Tiff took the orders and left. I introduced everyone to M1.

"What type of name is M1?" questioned Ciera.

"Yeah, what does that stand for?" asked Erica.

"It stands for Mack Daddy Number 1. You ain't heard?" M1 told 'em.

They looked at him like he was crazy.

"Nah, I'm just playing wit' y'all. M1 is a type of gun."

"I know your mother didn't name you after no gun. So what is your real name?" questioned Ciera, who was obviously digging my nigga.

"Damn, what you, da police? Let me check you for wires."

She laughed, but he was probably only half joking.

The drinks came back.

"Let me see your feet, l'il momma," I told Amelia.

She looked at me like she was confused, "Why?"

"Cause if your feet ugly, I can't fuck with you," I replied.

"You got me messed up. I don't have ugly feet," she said as she lifted her foot towards me.

"Oh, you tightwork. I see you with ya l'il French."

"Where you from? What you do?" I inquired.

She took a sip from her drink and responded, "I'm from here. I'm 26. I'm in law school at UM, and I intern for a law firm downtown."

"Oh, so you're almost a lawyer. Specializing in what?"

"Civil law. So what about you, Mr. 'All Black,' let me see your feet. What do you do?"

"Me, I'm an entrepreneur. I have a few business investments throughout the city. And I'm into international finance."

I hit her with my memorized bio.

"That's interesting. How old are you?" she asked.

"I'm 23."

"Quit lying. You seem older than that. You're mature for your age," she complimented.

"Does that mean that we can get further acquainted so that I can show you some of my other good qualities?" I asked seductively.

"That means I'm open minded and would be very interested in finding out what other qualities you have to offer," she replied, just as seductively.

Me and M1 ended up having drinks with lots of women. We had a lot of fun and, most importantly, we got a lot of numbers. If I could motivate M1, and sometimes I did, then I could even get him to talk up some accounts from the girls he hollered at.

Who says you can't mix business with pleasure?

CHAPTER 7

JAP
SATURDAY, 10 AM

My eyes opened. I lay on my back until the mush in my head began to function. The clock on the wall said 10:00 a.m. I could see the sun shining through the windows. The house was quiet. I got up and walked around. Everyone was gone. On the weekend, we alternated between taking Jr. to one of our parents' houses. So I knew she'd probably taken him to her mom's. She'd be out and about, so I'd call and check on her.

I grabbed my cell phone off the living room table and turned it on. I had messages, so I called and checked.

"Fuck," I meant to go get that damn work from Trap. That nigga done left 'bout five messages.

I dialed his number. It rang and rang – no answer. "I'll put on some clothes and go around there," I thought.. I called wifey.

"Hello," she answered.

"Wuz up, baby? Where you at?"

"I'm riding with Trenice. I just dropped Jr. off at my mother's house. Now we're going to get our hands and feet done."

"Aight. Well, I'm finna get dressed and go handle that business I was supposed to handle yesterday," I pushed out, with a slight attitude.

"Why you said it like that? I told you to go," I could hear the grin in her voice.

"You act like you were stuck or something."

"Man, whateva. I'll holla later." I hung up.

She won't call be back to back like she did yesterday cause she out and about with her homegirl. So she ain't thinking about me now.

I went and got dressed. On my way to Trap crib in Liberty City, I thought about how I didn't handle business yesterday. It might seem like a small issue to some, but small issues become big. So you nip 'em in da bud first. Plus, I'd bet those some ain't never had to chase down no "spare checks" to bust a bank account. Even Chill, with all his females and fun, handled business. He was disciplined. This was the first time I'd let my wife manipulate me to this extent. Short of an emergency with her or my shorty, business was supposed to be handled.

I pulled up at Trap house.

"What up, boy?" He opened the door and let me in.

"Ain't nothin', fool. What dey do?"

Trap was a gopher-type nigga. He worked at Publix Warehouse and stayed gambling. He was my wife's best friend's, Trenice, cousin. I met him at a get-together at Trenice's house over a year ago. We had bust his account, and after he ran through the money, he wanted to know how he could get more. So I told him. One thing I gotta admit is, in spite of his faults, the nigga kept some hoes. He'd brought plenty accounts to be worked and plenty of checks to be used.

"I see you called a couple hours ago. I was in there knocked out. I was up at the gambling house all night. Them niggas peeled my head back."

I chuckled, "Yeah, so I know you need these hot l'il two dollars."

"I damn sho do. I need to bounce back. But, my nigga, I ain't got da work."

"What you mean, fool? You told me you had it. What happen to it?"

"My nigga, I called you about ten times. I left five or six messages on ya pipe. You ain't answer, my nigga. I ain't know what da fuck happened. Them cats started raping me on da tonk table, and…"

Dis nigga doing too much explaining. He must've done some flaw shit.

"Aight, so what that go to do wit' da work?" I asked, confused.

"I got rid of it, my nigga."

"You got rid of it? What you mean you got rid of it? I don't understand." I was getting aggravated.

"I sold them shits to Rouseau. I was tryin' to get back. Shit, I thought you ain't want 'em no mo. You told me you was coming two times and didn't come. Then you wasn't answerin' ya pipe. You ain't eva did dat, my nigga. If you say you coming, you come, or at least call and say something. I thought you were duckin' a nigga and didn't want to tell me you ain't want 'em no more.

"Damn, homeboy, if I ain't want 'em, I would've told you I ain't want 'em, my nigga. Why you ain't hold them shits 'till today? I already knew the answer.

"What I'm supposed to do, dawg. Chase you around? I called you for hours, my nigga. My whole paycheck got took. I needed them chips. Dat's da only reason I sold 'em to ya cousin."

As much as I wanted to blame him, I couldn't.

"Yeah, I feel you, my nigga," I said dejectedly. "That's on me, you know what I'm saying. Early bird gets da worm. I respect game."

"If you woulda told me anything or answered da pipe and told me to hold it 'till today, that's what I woulda did."

"Don't worry about it," I acted nonchalant.

I really needed that work. But thinkin' 'bout it, something else was botherin' me.

"I'm say though, how Rou even know you had dat shit in da first place?"

He stretched his eyes and started scratching his head.

"Dat's on me, Jap," he said as he looked down," I was standing outside, calling you, and when you ain't answer, I started cussing out loud. Rou and one of his homeboys was out there and heard me. Rou asked me what was wrong, and…"

He paused.

"And what?" I prompted.

"And I guess because I was hot at you and I had lost my money I kind of advertised I had it," he looked up.

"But you told Rou that I was suppose to cop 'em from you first?"

"Yeah, I told 'em dat. I know y'all don't speak. I ain't mean to put da nigga in yo game room, my nigga."

"So he bought those from you. I know he asked you 'bout some more. I know my cousin. So what you told 'em?"

"I ain't tell 'em nothin'. That it was a one-time thing cause I'm locked in wit' you. He tried to cut you out, but I let him know it ain't going down like dat."

This nigga couldn't even look me in my eyes when he said that.

"Aight. Well, then, shit, just fuck wit' me when you come cross something else," I gave him dap and left.

I felt bad cause I didn't handle business. Once again, I felt like my wife sometimes held be back. We normally have spare check copies to use cause we collect 'em even when we don't need 'em. But when the Christmas season came through a couple months ago, we was boomin'. So now all we had was a bunch of dirty (used) checks. I had a bank account to bust, plus I know Chill had one. Both of them were supposed to start Monday. I hate screwups!

Even more, when I'm da one who's screwed up.

CHAPTER 8

CHILL
SATURDAY, 1 P.M.

We had a hell of a time last night, but it's back on da grind. I gotta take this young lady out to dinner. She's a potential client. Her name is Cecilia. I met her in the middle of the week while me and my son were at Chuck-E-Cheese. She was there with her 5-year-old daughter. She's twenty-eight and a dentist's assistant. Yeah, she has a beautiful smile, too. She's about 5'5, petite, and chocolate brown – from St. Thomas. She put you in the mind frame of Naomi Campbell, except she was more down to earth and her body was more wholesome. She had natural beauty, no makeup, short manicured nails and small, pretty, pedicured feet.

I like the weekends cause that's when my ol' girl (mom) is off from work. I can pick up my son and head over to my ol' girl's house. Although my mom was a single parent, my ol' boy was still around. I came from a middle-class family. When I first got on the block, niggas used to wonder why. I always answered, "I thug it 'cause I want to, not 'cause I have to." It's really in my blood. I have three cousins and one brother in the FED, uncles that used to grind when they were younger before they got strung out, and an aunt that pushed weight. So, although my ol' boy and ol' girl were career people, this shit chose me; I didn't choose it.

———

"What up, ma?" I asked, as I used my key to enter. DJ ran to his grandma, who he called "Mimi." She thinks the word grandma makes her sound old.

"Nothing. Sitting here watching my stories."

She tapes her soap operas while she's at work; then watches them on the weekends.

"Hey, man," they hugged. "You look so cute in your little outfit."

This was her firstborn grandchild.

"My daddy took me to Chuck-E-Cheese, Mimi."

"He did?! Did you have fun?"

He nodded his head, "Yesss."

She looked up at me, "So what have you been up to, Mante?"

"Same stuff, different day. Just makin' it. You know me."

"Yeah, I do. I also know you need to stop messing with all those women and get you one."

"There you go! Ma, you know there ain't no women out there that can understand me except you."

"Shiiit, you think I'd sit around while you chased women and use work as an excuse. You must be crazy."

I laughed.

"There you go. That's why I can't have no woman, only friends."

"Stop doing what you doing and you can," she scolded.

"Right, just give me a few more years and I'll settle down, ma."

"What's a few more years, Mante?"

"Umm... 'bout when I'm forty," I smirked.

———

I left my ol' girl house to head out to west Broward County to my main residence. It was about 3:00 p.m. I wanted to check on the house and get dressed. Plus, Cecilia lived in Sunrise, not too far away. I lived in a gated neighborhood called Crestwater Estates. I'd purchased my home directly from the owner. I'd went around the realtor. I checked property records on the internet and, essentially, cut out the middle man. We had a win/win situation. He didn't have to pay commission fees and I paid the owner directly and didn't have the FED's on my ass.

It was a two-story, recently built house, as in the last five years. The house was sitting on a lake. The bottom floor had an industrial-sized kitchen with the appliances to match. In addition to the living room, full dining room, family room, two bathrooms and a screened-in patio, upstairs had two guest bedrooms with an attached bathroom in the middle and a master bedroom with a sitting room Jacuzzi, and a balcony overlooking the lake. It was valued at $450,000 when I bought it. But with all the new people moving in, and shopping centers being built, I knew the value was steadily appreciating. I am super blessed.

I don't take anything for granted.

———

"So tell me about yourself, sweetie," I told Cecilia.

We were sitting in a restaurant called Legal Seafood, in Sunrise, near the world-famous Sawgrass Mills Mall.

"I don't know. What do you want to know?"

"I wanna know about you. Tell me your do's and don'ts, your maybes and won'ts. I wanna know what turns you on and off." I eyed her directly.

She sat back, smiled, and watched me sexily.

"I know some things I'll have to learn on my own, but I wouldn't mind a little head start."

She grinned.

"Ok, well, how about we make a deal. For every fact I tell you, you tell me one. That way I don't feel like I'm talking too much," she replied.

"Alright, sweetie, I'm with that. So what made you wanna play in people's mouths?" I joked.

"Well, actually, it came from when I used to go to the dentist as a little girl. I used to have so much fun, you know, with the bubble gum fluoride and the lollipop thing. I guess I'm weird because I actually used to look forward to going to the dentist. And I know my dentist used to be like, "Oh, Lord, here comes that aggravating little girl who asks all those damn questions."

We laughed.

"It doesn't sound weird. It sounds like it was your destiny."

"I know, right. Same thing my mom says. Ok, your turn. How did you get into international finance?"

"Well, I always felt like the world was bigger than the US. I've always liked to explore. And being that the US dollar is worth more in a lot of countries, it's amazing how you can invest in third world or other countries and find value in things you normally wouldn't over here. To be able to bank and play with foreign currency is fun for me." I ran it down.

"And you say you're only twenty-five. Um, I'm scared of you, Mr. Man," she smiled.

"So what's up with you and your child's father?"

"We broke up about two years ago, and I've been single ever since. Going to school, working, and raising Gabrielle pretty much keeps me occupied."

"I know, it gets hard for you to do all that, you know what I'm saying. My hat goes off to you. You're a strong woman," I complimented.

She blushed, "Thank you! You're so sweet. And, yes, it gets rough. I almost had to quit school this semester for financial reasons, until I got a loan from my bank. But you gotta do what you gotta do."

I looked at her admiringly, but I was really only pleased with the last statement: account.z

———

"It's still early, only 7:40. I don't want you to get the wrong impression, but would you like to come up and finish talking or watch a movie? Oh, I'm sorry. Do you have something else to do?"

"Naw, I don't, sweetie. Actually, I've been enjoying the evening, and I'd hate to let it end so soon."

We climbed the stairs to her apartment. The whole time I was trying to figure out what approach I was going to use to achieve my goal.

"You have a nice apartment. It's comfortable."

"Thank you. That's another passion of mine, interior decorating. I like to take little knickknacks and match them together."

"Shit, based on what I'm seeing, I'd pay you to decorate my crib."

"Oh, yeah, where is your house?"

"I have a home in Carol City, down in Miami. Just a l'il two-bedroom bachelor pad."

I told a quick lie.

"I have an aunt in C.C. Would you like something to drink?"

"Yeah, whatever type of juice you have will be fine. What kind of DVDs are you working with?"

"I have 'The Titanic.' Do you like movies like that?"

(Fuck no)

"Yeah, let's check it out."

———

"Do you like the movie, or is it boring you?" She asked me, knowingly.

"I'm good, sweetie. Besides, whether the movie was boring or not," I looked at her sitting next to me on the couch, "I'm happy just being around you," I spit out, innocently.

She smiled and watched me like she was struggling with a decision. She finally said, "There's something about you that makes me feel real comfortable. You make me feel like I've known you for years. It's like I can relax and say things to you and don't feel self conscious about anything," she confided.

"Sweetie, just be yourself. 'Cause I'm gonna be me regardless. I mean, like, for instance, I don't want you to think I'm being mannish or aggressive, but I wanna kiss you. Can I?"

She turned sideways on the couch facing me. She gazed at me intently, smirked, and raised one eyebrow.

"I don't know. Can you?"

Say no more!

I leaned over and cupped her chin between my thumb and forefinger. I kissed her softly, leaned back, and saw the passion dancing in her eyes. I responded by kissing her slowly, deliberately. Our tongues slow-danced, as one hand stroked the back of her neck and the other held her hand. I took her hand and placed it around my neck and, while I nibbled on her chin, planted baby kisses along her neck and sucked on her earlobe.

"Ummm," she moaned.

I whispered in her ear, "Tell me if you want me to stop."

"Boy, don't play," she whispered back, grabbed my neck tighter, and lay back on the couch. I continued to explore her body with my hands and mouth. I was a little kid and her body was my playground. My tongue tickled her navel and danced around her nipples while my fingers provided teasing feather-strokes around the lips of her inner sanctum.

I nibbled and kissed my way up the inside of her thighs and sucked firmly behind her kneecaps. I blew air on her moist treasure just to let it know I was there. Her back arched and she bit her bottom lip in response to my tongue parting her pink folds. Her hips bucked wildly against my face when I squeezed her clit firmly between my lips and licked my name on it. Her body shivered as I drank in the river of her essence.

"Ssss. I want you inside of me. Ssss, mmmm, please," she shivered.

"Tell me again," I said, as I rubbed my sheathed sword up and down the entrance of her tunnel of bliss.

She stared deeply into my eyes, "Pl...pl...please put it in me. I need to feel you inside me," she pushed down on my buttocks and opened her legs wider.

I could feel the heat engulf me as I entered the depths of her lust.

Stroke for stroke.

I was an artist, and her body was my canvas.

Our bodies were a collage of fantasy, eroticism and ecstasy.

But I wasn't making love. I was making money!

CHAPTER 9

SUNDAY, AROUND 1 P.M.

"I'm on da way to da ol' girl house now, fool," I told Jap.

"Right, I'll meet you there," he replied.

"You gonna meet me there? What, Shay gonna actually let you out the house? Hold up. Let me look up in da sky and see if pigs flyin' and shit," I taunted.

We laughed.

"Fuck you, Chill. I move when I wanna move. Plus, she had to work today."

"Now it make sense. Nigga, you sneakin'."

"Nigga, I'm grown."

"Hey, my other line ringin'. Just fall through. DJ and I will be there."

"Right, I'll holla."

I clicked over.

"Hello?"

"Hey, you. Are you busy?"

"I'm not ever too busy for you, Cecilia."

"You better stop. I could get use to this kind of treatment."

"I wouldn't have it any other way," I responded.

"So why haven't you called me yet?"

"As a matter of fact, I was. I was giving it 'til after two. That's when most people get out of church. So how are you and your daughter doing?"

Well, I got out of church at eleven. I went to early service. My daughter and I are fine. We're at my grandmother's. What about you?"

"I'm on the way to my momma's house now, to eat and chill. But, listen, I've been thinking about you all day."

"Aww, that's so sweet. Have you really?"

I rolled my eyes.

"Yes, I have, and I need to talk to you about something. I would like to help you out a little with your financial difficulties."

"Ohhh, you don't have to do that."

"Well, if I can help, sweetie, then I can help. You know? So I'll talk to you about it later."

"Ok, that's fine."

"So have a nice day, sweetie."

"You too, and thanks for last night."

―――

"So what happened now?"

Jap and I were standing in the backyard at my ol' girl house smoking a joint rolled out of Backwood.

"I fucked up and didn't go pick up dat work from Trap."

I hit the joint and listened.

"I let Shay stop me from doing business, fool. That's on me, my nigga. I fucked up."

I was more annoyed than pissed.

"You know I don't get into ya marriage issues, dawg. That ain't my place. But when it starts interfering with ya work ethic, then I gotta say somethin', my nigga. We ain't hurtin' fa chips by a long shot. But you know I got that account from dat l'il broad, Regina, and you got one..."

"I already know, fool. I know what you thinking. But I ain't even finished yet."

"DJ, stop standing up in dat swing 'fore you fall!" I yelled at my son.

I passed Jap da joint.

"What? There's more?. Mannn, somethin' tellin' me this shit gonna be crazy! Let me sit down."

"'Member I told you 'bout da nigga gamblin' habit, right?"

I nodded my head.

"Da nigga lost his paycheck and sold da work to Rou!"

"He sold da work to Rou? How da fuck Rou know he got work?"

"He approached Rou after he called me and I had my phone off. He…"

"Hold up, hold up, hold up. Damn dawg, you cut off yo phone, my nigga?. How da fuck you gonna handle business with your phone off, Jap? You got this man waiting on you and you cut yo phone off. You trippin', for real. I woulda sold that shit, too."

I walked over to play with da kids on da playground I put up in my ol' girl's backyard. Playin' wit da kids relaxes me and I makes me think clearly. I played wit' them for about thirty minutes. While I was playin' and thinkin', Jap sat in da screened-in patio thinkin' about da errors of his ways.

"You know what, homeboy? We got to find a better way to get paperwork. All this depending on Trap and chasing people to make copies of they checks is a hassle. We need a more reliable and steady means."

"I feel ya. I was just thinkin' da same shit," Jap replied.

"Not even just that. What happens when we can't get work or we're waiting on work, but it ain't payday. So now, every time, we gonna have to take a pause. You know, just like I know that when you hold people's shit for too long, dey change they minds."

"Yeah, they either end up talking to someone or thinkin' too much."

"Right, so now that account you got; you picked it up today. I've been holdin' mine since Thursday. We both promised them we'd start tomorrow. When we tell 'em there's a delay, to them, it's gonna look unprofessional. They gonna start gettin' second thoughts."

"There ain't nothin' wrong wit' a l'il break." responded Jap.

"True. But we usually take our breaks during da summer months. I don't mind breakin', but I'd rather break when we want to instead of 'cause we have to."

"Dawg, you ain't gotta worry about me fuckin' up no more. Shay wanna live this good life and have all da accessories that come wit' it, then she gotta understand."

"But it's more than that, homeboy. This shit is just a wake-up call. We need a betta way."

"What you got in mind, Chill?"

"We need a connect inside one of these damn banks. Instead of that fugazi-ass shit we be shootin' to everyone."

"It sound good, but it's easier said than done. Shit, we already knew we could use an inside connect."

"Yeah, but this situation just made me realize how much more critical it is. Now we got this Rouseau in our game room. Ain't no telling what him and Trap been talkin' 'bout."

"Nah fool, that was a one-time thing. I slipped and Rou gripped. It won't happen again."

"Dawg, don't be naive. You know, just like I know that nigga, Rou is slicker than a can of oil, my nigga. I don't put shit past no nigga, especially since I know da nigga got beef for us as it is."

I was gettin' heated.

"Soft ass nigga act like a nigga owe him somethin'. He got short-term memory. He gonna make me remind his ass!"

"Nah, we good. Let's just continue wit' our plans. We ain't gonna let nothin' get in our way."

"Ain't nothin' gonna get in our way regardless, and you can bet da bank on that!"

———

"Ma, we finna get ready to leave."

"Ok, drive safe. Come give Mimi a hug, DJ."

He ran over, still full of energy.

"So you're going to take him home?"

"Daddy, I want to go to your house."

"You might as well take him to your house and take him to school in the morning."

"I might just keep him the whole week. I might not have to work."

"DJ, you wanna stay with me all week?"

"Yesss," he shook his head.

"Give Mimi a kiss and you can stay with daddy all week."

"Ok, daddy. Mimi, I give you a big kiss." He kissed her cheek.

"Alright, ma, I'll call you tomorrow. We might drive to your job and take you to lunch."

"Well, that would be a treat. Y'all got your plates?"

"Oh, you know we ain't leaving no food, ma!"

"I know, that's right."

"I'm gone. Love you, ma."

"Love you too."

CHAPTER 10

JAP
APRIL

It has been a slow two months. Me and Chill had to take an unscheduled break from work. Thinking back on what he said a couple months ago, he was right. We do need an inside connect, 'cause paperwork has been scarce. Even if we met a new person everyday, which I know Chill did, it was still work to make someone give you a copy of their check. For all the game in the world you spit, some people just ain't with it. Unfortunately, those are the types we've run into. If we could at least find a couple of people with accounts, who also worked, we could mix and match; use one check on the other's account. But the last seven accounts we grabbed, all seven were in the negative or were in the negative recently enough to affect the outcome of the account. Plus, they were all in between jobs, and two were strippers, so they didn't have no paycheck anyway.

I see now what a luxury it was to have that nigga Trap out there rounding them up for us. 'Cause I don't care what fool say, once we went over that quarter-mil mark, we were still hungry. Don't get it twisted; but it's a different kind of hunger. Trap finally came clean about him and Rou's l'il business deal. I can't hate. Any nigga would do the same shit. Yeah, we could outdo Rou's price. But I ain't finna make a nigga feel we counting on him like that.

So fuck 'em and feed 'em fish. But I know we're going to have to go see our accountant this week and get a check on our finances. I know we been smart. So I know we can coast a l'il bit, but not too much. Cause the more money we started making, the more bills we accumulated. I know I spend between five and ten grand on bills each month, not including miscellaneous shit. Even though Chill ain't married, I know his bills are almost double mine, with a mortgage on the "Play Pad" and "The Big House."

In the meantime, my wife has gotten plenty used to me being at home. I must admit that we have been gettin' along quite well. But I already know that as soon as things pick back up, she's going to start crabbin' again. But I'll cross that bridge when I get to it. For now, I'm gonna milk it for all its worth. We finally got a chance to take a l'il vacation. We went on a ten-day cruise. We hit seven islands and countries. It felt like old times. It feels real nice to have a l'il harmony. To be honest, I'm not in any rush to end it. But she has to work and so must I.

"What up, fool?" I spoke, as Chill answered the phone.

"Ain't nothin'. Just chillin' out at the big house."

"What's new on yo end?"

"We have an appointment with Lauren on Thursday."

"Aight, cool. What time?"

"Three p.m. sharp. So be on point. I'll meet you there, cause prior to our engagement, I'm having lunch with a nice young lady."

"Oh, yeah? Somethin' in da works?"

"Ain't nothin' major, just keepin' my skills sharp. Man, I hope the Heat don't lose this game. I got too much cash on this shit."

"Don't end up like Trap. You'll be sellin' ya jewelry," I joked.

"One thing 'bout it, fool; I'll be back to da basics, robbin' and selling dope 'fo I go broke, homeboy. Speakin' of which, what's up wit' dat nigga, anyway?"

"He still vibin' wit Rou. I ain't hollered at the nigga in a minute. I seen 'em at Trenice house when me and Shay went a couple weeks ago, but dat's about it."

"I don't know about you, but I got some plans for big Rouseau and them!"

"What you got in mind?" I questioned curiously.

"You just sit back and be family guy. Let me handle this gangsta nigga."

"Whateva, nigga. I can get gutta too!" I stated defensively.

"Nigga, da only time you gutta is when you take da trash out," I laughed. "But I'll see you Thursday, big homey. I gotta finish watching dis game. If I cross my fingers and toes, they might pull it off. I'll holla," he hung up.

I wondered what he had in mind. Knowing my nigga and how manipulative he is, it was something real slimy. Shit, I can't wait to see. Now, where the hell was Shay? She was supposed to be back over an hour ago. I'm hungry as shit. If it woulda been me, she'd be ready to kill me.

SHAY

"You sure you have to leave already?" he asked.

"Already? I was supposed to be home a long time ago," I told him.

"I know. I just don't like to let you leave when I'm around you," replied fuck buddy.

"I want to stay too. You got my body feeling so good right now. My pussy is so wet," I told him, as I lay naked on top of the covers.

"Let me taste it. I'll make you nut again real quick!"

"Uh-uh, I gotta... um, shit, boy. You're gonna get me in trou... Fuck, suck, mom – pus – ummm!"

I left the hotel fifteen minutes later, sore and happy.

CHAPTER II

CHILL
THURSDAY, 3PM

"What's up, fellas? Long time no see," Lauren greeted us, as she give us each a hug. "You guys don't even call or come by the house like you used to."

"I don't think your boyfriend like us. I think he feels like you have something going on with one of us," I said with a smirk.

"Yeah, dat nigga act phony as a muhfucka when we do come 'round or call," Jap cut in.

"So we don't want you to have any conflicts on the home front because of us," I explained.

"Don't worry about that. You guys are my friends and always will be. Boyfriends come and go, but not true friends. So if he can't accept that, then he knows where the door is!" She looked at me.

"Besides, D'mante, I'm just passing time with him until you decide you want to settle down." I smiled; she didn't.

We were at her office in Coral Gables. Lauren is one of my mother's closest friend's daughter. My mother and her mother had been friends forever. When I was younger, I had a crush on her. Shit, I still did. But I didn't want to spoil the fruit and ruin our friendship over bullshit – my bullshit. I knew I wasn't ready and she was. She always had been.

Lauren was eight years older than I was. She was from Guyana and had a beautiful Indian complexion. Her hair was stylishly cut short around slanted Heineken bottle-green eyes, high cheekbones, and lips like Angelina Jolie's. At 5'6", 145 pounds, and slant legged, she was a goddess. Plus, she had some of the prettiest feet I ever saw. You could put them in a magazine.

Her mother worked for one of the most prestigious law firms in Miami. She passed on her connects and some tricks to her daughter, who was a highly respected and well connected accountant and financial advisor. Jump started by her mother's reputation and kept intact by her shrewd skills, her clientele ran the gamut from businessmen and politicians to athletes and entertainers. But, despite her success, she looked at us like family and we looked at her the same way.

"I didn't realize that I was so humorous," she shot back.

"Nah, I ain't laughing. I'm blushing," I responded.

Jap sat and watched our sparring. He was used to it.

"You know the only reason I even bother with you, D'mante. I know you're young and still wanna do your thing. But I also know how you feel about me. You don't have to tell me, cause I see it in your eyes. I know you don't want to hurt me. I respect that," she eyed me intently.

"I've had marriage proposals, baby proposals. Even a well-known entertainer offered me one million dollars to marry him for two years. But that's not what I want. So I won't sacrifice my happiness or settle for anything else. You know why?" she asked.

She was the only girl who could tie my tongue. I couldn't talk, so I just raised my eyebrows.

"Because you are what makes me happy, D'mante. So enjoy yourself and get it all out of your system. I know you won't forget about me. Your heart won't let you." She switched gears, "With that said, let's get down to business."

Sure, nice way to start after you fuck my head up.

We were seated in her office, twenty stories above the City of Coral Gables.

"You first, Jap. The value of your portfolio, including your stockholdings as of closing time yesterday, bonds, mutual funds, CD's and," she looked up at him and smiled, "your offshore account that Shay doesn't know about, your NAV (net asset value) is $162,481.19," she looked up once again.

"That's excluding my condo and cars, right?" Jap asked.

"Correct. You told me not to include them, so I didn't. As you know, all of your bills are paid directly from LEM Corporation, the shell company I created for you, overseas. You are employed by them. They wire your bank, and your bank pays your bills. But you know all this."

"Damn, gettin' kind of low, ain't it?"

"Well, by your standards, yes. By the average person's standards, no," she answered.

"Yeah, I feel you. It's just that the last few months I've been spending and spending without bringin' in any income. I didn't realize how far down I'd gotten. I spent close to thirty stacks on that trip Shay and I took. Then, every-day living," Jap explained.

"Well, if you guys are having a dry spell, you have to expect that. Every company has dry spells, except Microsoft," she joked. "Just watch your spend-ing. Cut down until things pump back up. Let Shay know she has to lay off the designer handbags and clothes for a minute. You'll be ok. So don't panic. As for the trip you took, bring me the receipts. I can write it off under LEM as a busi-ness expense – networking and promotional tour," she winked and smiled.

"I'm good," he looked at me, "just ready to crank back up and get this money."

I nodded my head.

"I'll let y'all talk. I have to get back on da NW side to pick up Jr. from day-care. I don't wanna get stuck in traffic."

"How is l'il Jap? I know he's getting so big," Lauren inquired.

"Oh, he's good. Eatin' everything in sight," Jap responded.

"Fool, holla at me later on. I'll be at home," he said to me.

"Fa sho. I'll get at you."

"See you later, Lauren."

She came around the desk and gave him a hug.

"Ok, Jap. Don't be a stranger."

She opened the office door, let him out, and closed it.

"Now, Mr. Chill, she said as she walked back around her desk and sat down.

"Let's look at our finances," she looked up. "Yes, I said *our* finances. I have to take extra special care of you, honey. Because your future is my future."

I smiled. I was sincerely touched that a woman outside of my family could care about me so much. She smiled back as if she read my thoughts.

"You're not in a hurry, are you?" She slipped off her shoes,. "As we have a lot to discuss."

"Nah, I cleared my schedule because this is highly important, and I didn't know how long it would take," I explained.

"Good. Let's start with your tangible possessions. The "Big House," as you guys call it, has almost doubled in appreciation, now valued at $750,000. Your jewelry is appraised at $200,000, and your car is valued at $100,000 – but you that depreciates every year, especially with the extras you've added. I have receipts for over $150,000 in furnishings. Counting depreciation, you figure they're worth half that amount. Including cash, your NAV puts you at well over a million in assets."

"But if you're just counting monetary assets, then you've got a little over a quarter million at $256,832.04. That's cash, stocks, CDs and bonds." She looked up and sat back. "Baby, I'm proud of you. You've come a long way in just the two years you've been home."

"Thank you. Your opinion means a lot to me. God forbid, but if I ran into any problems with the crackas, I'd be ok, right? I mean I put enough contingencies in place in case of an emergency, right?"

"I would say so, yes. I might say a little overboard. But you can never be too cautious. I mean we've set up, at last count, fourteen dummy companies in six different foreign countries. The board of directors names match the IDs, passports, and work citizenship VISAs that you and I have. Plus, we have offshore accounts that tie directly to those companies."

"So, none of those tie back to us. But, if for some unforeseen reason, the government started digging, it would be years before they made it through just the first account and business. All the countries we've used either have a non-enforced or non-existent NAFTA agreement with the US. The red tape surrounding that is damn near insurmountable or years to get around at best. By that time, *we*, and I repeat *we*, would be out of the country in Argentina or Peru or somewhere. And those funds would jump through fifteen or twenty different countries with one phone call, making them untraceable.

"The only company that ties back to you is the Diempur Corporation, on the Isle of Curaco, which as you know, you're on the payroll as the Executive Vice President of sales," Lauren explained.

"Thanks, sweetie. Everything sounds like it's on point. I just want to make sure things are copacetic."

"Why, baby?" Are you having bad vibes? If worse comes to worse, you still have plan B – your numbered accounts on the Isle of Mann. They have strict confidentiality laws and no agreement whatsoever with the good ol' US of A. So we're ok, baby! But you know you can also just stop cold and do something else. I'll help you in whatever you want to do. I have your back," she assured.

"I'm not having bad thoughts; just mapping things out in my head and want to stay on point. Rest assured, l'il momma, I have your back, too – always!" She blushed.

"Even if you marry someone else." She stopped smiling and came around the desk. She bent over me and grabbed my face with two hands.

"That's not how it works. I love you, and in my country, when you love someone, you give your life to them. Don't worry about hurting me. I know deep inside how you feel. Trust me. In the meantime, just appreciate me and respect me, and we'll be fine." She kissed me firmly on the lips.

I'd be damn fool to fuck that up, which is a Shame, because I probably will!

"Mante, when is my birthday?" she stood over me and asked sweetly. I frowned, wondering what this has to do with anything.

"June sixth," I answered. "Why?"

"I'm just checking, making sure you know. But I'm having a party at the penthouse and you better be there and bring Jap. There's going to be a lot of people there for you to network and expand your horizons. A lot of people who I want you to meet – people you *need* to meet."

"You know I'll already be there. It's gonna be a hell of a time getting Jap out the house, but I'll try."

"L'Shay still has him under lock and key, huh?"

"Yeah, you know how that goes. I try not to get into it unless it fucks with business. In this case, I may just tell him to bring her."

"Well, that's not a problem. How is your mom and my little booboo?"

"They're both alright. Everyone's healthy and blessed."

"And how are you?"

"I'm ok."

"No, I mean really, baby. How are you?"

"Honestly? I don't know. I really haven't taken time to get in touch with myself lately. I've just been focusing on business and money. Things have been slow, and I'm working on a way to fix them."

"Come here," she grabbed me by the hand and led me over to her leather couch, sat me down and stood behind me.

"You know you always have to take self time or you'll burn yourself out. You have to take time to reflect on where you've come from, where you are now, and where you're headed next," she told me in a soothing voice as she massaged my neck.

I sat back with my eyes closed.

"Don't ever get caught up so much in this world where it starts to weigh on your spirit. Your spirit collects negativity and you have to constantly cleanse it. When you have eyeglasses, and they get dirty, you have to cleanse them or you lose sight. It's the same with your spirit – you collect so much dirt until you lose sight of all the good within yourself. Baby, your spirit is strong. It's a warrior. But even the strongest warriors must replenish and nourish themselves or they'll falter on their journey."

"Health is not all about physicality and muscle. You have to be mentally and spiritually healthy as well. All three go hand in hand."

I guess it was her island roots, but she always got this way when she was concerned for me. She could always pick up on vibes and energy, good or bad. I believed in stuff like that, but it was always amazing to see it done.

"Baby, you have a lot of negative thoughts and energy surrounding you. Whatever your intentions are in the next couple of weeks, be careful because they could cause you and Jap serious, even terminal, problems."

She pulled my head back and looked in my eyes.

"I'm not gonna ask you what's going on. I respect your privacy. But, please, listen to me, baby." She kissed my forehead, then my nose, and my mouth.

"I hear you, Lauren. I always take heed to what you say. Shit, half the time you say bad shit and have me scared as a muhfucka anyway." I said, trying to make light of the situation.

"Gee, I hope I make you feel good the other half of that time," she said inquisitively.

"You always make me feel good, even when you scare me," I said sincerely.

"I know," she shot back and kissed me again. "You make me feel good inside, too."

"I love you," were my only thoughts.

She walked in front of me, looked deeply in my Eyes, and said, "I love you, too, Mante'," she smiled.

When I left Lauren's office, I actually did feel better. But momma always said I was hardheaded. She was right. I did have some negative thoughts with a negative plan to match.

I just hope my spirit had a l'il more room left for all the negativity it was gonna collect.

Lauren had put a lot on my mind, and I pondered as I headed over to da Leaf to meet up with M1. But what I came up with so far was dat nigga Rouseau had some beef on his chest. We hadn't fucked with dude in two years, but the way him and Jap fell out, I felt like he thought a nigga owe him somethin'. That's why he was quick to jump on the band wagon with Trap. Dat's okay, ol' hoe-ass nigga. Da Bible says "turn the other cheek," but it also says "an eye for an eye". And dat's the shit I'm on!

————

I watched all da young niggas playin' da cut, gettin dat money. The young niggas M1 had out here grindin' was da same l'il niggas dat used to watch us when we were fifteen, sixteen, seventeen. They were like ten, eleven, twelve, lookin' up to us. . Now it's dey turn to come out da house. This shit here is a cycle. One minute you taking all da kids to da ice cream truck. For those of us who ain't left somewhere stank or in jail, the cycle continues.

I got out da whip and gave M1 and da rest of da l'il goons dap.

"What dey do, fellas?" I called out.

"What up, boy?" M1 hollered. "I see you low-key today."

I was rollin' in da Buick behind tints.

"What up, Chill?" cried out Chauncey. L'il nigga always looked up to me da most. When I was his age, I was beatin' (fuckin') his ol' girl, who was about thirty.

"What day do, Chaunce? I see you, Goon, and Taterhead, stackin' dem chips."

"Damn right! We tryin' to be like y'all was, CLB. We rep to da fullest, my nigga."

Dat shit made me smile.

"Y'all niggas be betta than us. That's how you rep. Take what you learn, plus you own experiences, and take shit to another level, ya feel me?" I preached.

"Teach them niggas later on, fool. Let's holla bout this business you was spittin' at a nigga," M1 said anxiously.

We headed over to his DL whip, a '98 Chevy Lumina, navy blue, wit' five percent tints. The nigga looked like them folks.

I jumped in.

"So what da beat is? Who done pissed my nigga off? It's been a long time since I saw it, but I know that look anywhere, nigga."

"We finna touch this nigga Rouseau," I answered.

"Rouseau? Jap cousin Rouseau?" he frowned. "You stop Tech and them from stankin' him so you can stank 'em yourself?"

"I ain't say we gonna lean da nigga. Although if it come to that, I don't have no qualms. I said we gonna touch 'em. We gonna fall off in that gambling house."

"Fool, I been wanted to do that. You spared that nigga on that, too. You an ol' merciful-ass nigga. I knew you was a part-time hero," he joked.

"It wasn't that. You know my mind don't work that way. I have to let shit marinate. My mind is analytical."

He looked at me crazy and said "Aight, 'Professor Chill'. Please don't tell me we have study and take SATs and shit to rob this nigga."

I turned and looked at him, "Nah, I already did that for us. I got it all mapped out. First things first, I need you to call you cousin, Pocahontas. Tell her we need her to holla at Spice, L'il Bit and three more girls. We need them to come down here da first week of next month."

"Da reason I say da first week is because May 1st is on a Wednesday. Checks will be poppin' off all week, niggas getting paid Friday from regular jobs. We let niggas eat all week and Friday. Dat Saturday, da fourth or Sunday, 'cause it'll be past midnight, we touch 'em. You know, it's gonna be super crowded with niggas playin' wit that job money and that sac money they been makin' from da first of da month?"

"Damn dawg, how long you been mappin' this one out? And how we gonna use da girls?"

"I been on that nigga ass since I heard he hollered at Trap on da sly. Now roll up a joint and listen while I give you da rest of da game."

CHAPTER 12

ROUSEAU

"Damn, my nigga, look at them hoes pullin' up in da Sebring," called out Zeek.

Rouseau squinted as the glare from the sun fucked with his vision.

Pocahontas, L'il Bit, and Spice pulled in, parked, and got out. It was crowded outside the car wash. And everyone was sweatin' the females in da Sebring – females and all! Poca and the girls knew it.

"Y'all just gonna stare at our car or y'all gonna put us in line?" asked Poca, as they walked towards the front of the building where most of the crowd was.

Black Dave yelled out, "L'il momma, we ain't staring at ya car, that's fa damn sho."

"I know that's right, my nigga," agreed Zeek.

"Well, what y'all lookin' at then? Ya see something y'all like?" asked L'il Bit sarcastically.

Rou stepped up, "Roscoe, pull that car up in line," then looked back at the threesome, "And we most definitely see a lot we like!"

Pocahontas had on an orange and gold Azure body- suit that stopped just below her ass cheeks. She is 5'6", 150 pounds, and high yellow, with a straw-set hairdo and Hennessey brown eyes, on a face that only God could have per- fected. She had a panther crawling up her left thigh, which were thick, flawless, and toned from working with a personal trainer. And her feet were standing in gold Jimmy Choo four-inch stilettos, with feet and hands painted gold.

L'il Bit is 5'1", 135 pounds, dark chocolate-roasted, and bowlegged. She had pretty white teeth and dimples, a small button nose, oriental dark brown eyes and her hair was styled in twists. Her body was oiled smooth, and fitted in a gray and pink Prada tennis skirt, shirt to match, and gray and pink casual Prada tennis shoes. She topped it off with the visor to match and Prada rimless, Smokey-gray tinted shades.

Spice is a Dominican Amazon. She is 5'10", 190 pounds with skin the color of dark Caribbean spices. She has wavy jet-black hair down to her ass; plus, she was built like an Arabian thoroughbred. She was clad tight in lavender and teal Chloe capri's with a matching formfitting halter top that stopped right above her bellybutton, which held a one carat diamond that glistened in the sun. Her calve muscles were well defined in matching Chloe high-heeled slip-ons.

"them hoes ain't all dat!" two female customers said amongst themselves, mad that the attention was taken away from them.

"How much y'all charge, kinfolk, for the work?" Poca asked Roscoe.

"Twelve dollars in and out. You left da keys inside?"

"Yeah," she answered.

"Kinfolk?" Dave frowned. "Niggas don't talk like that down here. Where y'all from?"

"We from Houston," answered Spice.

"What y'all doing down here?" Dave asked.

"Damn, touch your nose," L'il Bit said, with attitude and head movement. The fellas smiled.

"Nah, it ain't like that l'il momma. A nigga just curious," Dave said, embarrassed.

Poca looked at Rou, who she had been shown pictures of, and said, "We came down here to work."

"Work – what kind of work?" questioned Dave.

Everybody looked at him as if he was a dickhead.

"How long have y'all been down here so far?" I asked.

"We got here Thursday," responded Poca. "There's three more of us, but they stayed at the room."

Niggas eyes got big.

"Y'all came dee'd (packed) up ain't it?" spit out Zeek, tryin' to figure out how he could fuck something.

"We came to get money. So we bought our whole l'il clique," explained Spice.

"What y'all got lined up for tonight?" I inquired. The wheels in my head were spinning. How can I get in where I fit in?

"We did the Rolexx last night. It was straight. So we might go back. Or we heard CoCo's be poppin' on Saturdays," informed Poca.

"I got a betta idea," I chipped in. Damn, all three girls look at me skeptically, like I was nobody. Let me talk to the redbone. She seem like she is the leader. See if I can put the game down.

"Y'all two mind if I talk to your homegirl, solo?" I asked, while I eyed the other two for their reaction.

"Nigga, she grown, ask her!" stated L'il Bit with a slick tongue.

"You need a nigga to put that dick game down on you, make you civilized," Dave spit at L'il Bit.

"Ain't no nigga did it yet and you talk too much, so I know your dick little." Everyone laughed as I pulled l'il momma to the side.

"First off, l'il momma, I'm Rouseau. Niggas call me Rou for short," I held out my hand. She shook it but didn't respond.

"Damn, you ain't gonna tell me your name, sweetheart?"

"Oh, that's what you waiting on. I'm Pocahontas."

"What about your homegirls?"

"The short one is L'il bit, and the tall one is Spice."

"I gotta proposition for you. I just want you to hear me out."

"I'm listening now. So what's the deal, kinfolk?"

"Why don't y'all come through here later on tonight and get your grind on?" I explained, "Things get jumpin' around ten or eleven."

Poca laughed, "You want us to dance up here at your car wash?" She played dumb.

"Nah, l'il one. This is the gambling house, and y'all could make a killing up here. There's a few stragglers in there now, but the real action comes through after hours. Let me show you. Check me out." They walked through the waiting area to the closed garage section of the wash.

Inside, Rou had tonk tables set up and two pool tables for rolling Celo. It was about ten niggas in there rolling dice and playing cards. It was two flat screens on the walls and a couple of leather couches for lounging.

"So what you think?" I asked her. I could tell by her body language she was feeling the setup.

"Damn, this is nice. You're serious, huh?. Y'all got your little garage tricked out like somebody house. It's comfortable in here."

"Comfortable enough for y'all to work?" I asked her.

She nodded her head and smiled.

"I got it laid so niggas will stay and lose they chips. So I got everything a nigga need. I got da TVs so niggas can bet on Madden. One for the PS, the other for the Xbox. Late night is anywhere from forty to fifty niggas in here, all making and losing money." I let that sink in.

Now for part two. I'm gonna get paid off these hoes. I'm already countin' the chips.

"Sooo, I know you're not letting us dance for free. So what's the catch?" She looked at me, eye to eye. A real thoroughbred. I like that. I might try to lock her down.

"I want forty percent." She frowned. "Hold up and just listen first," I cut her off,. "By y'all dancing here, y'all are the main attraction. Y'all don't have any competition. Unlike the club, every nigga in here got money. So you ain't gotta waste your time trying to figure out who's broke and who's not. You guaranteed to eat."

Poca pretended to mull over the offer.

"Look, I guarantee y'all make two grand or better. I don't care what you say, no club can guarantee that outcome. I'm doing it for all six of y'all." I couldn't have ran it down no smoother than that, but I wasn't finished. "And unlike the club, I don't have a problem with y'all getting money on the side. You feel me? And y'all can keep all of that!" I smirked.

"Alright, you gotta deal, but..."

"But what?" I frowned and asked.

"But only if you agree that if we don't make two thousand a piece we don't have to pay nothing!" Now *she* smirked.

Damn! She good. I gots to fuck that. I'm pretty sure I can pull it off. Fuck it. Worse come to worse I don't lose shit and I get some good promotion.

"Aight, that's a deal. My people hold all the money. We wouldn't want anything to get lost in translation. On y'all's end, count it as y'all get it so y'all at least have an idea of the count."

"Deal," we shook on it.

"Come prepared to work!" we went back outside.

SUNDAY, 12:56 A.M.

"Hey, here come those l'il dancer hoes pulling up by the gate," Scrap yelled inside to me. I was sitting in my office with my gunman, Buddha.

I walked to my office door and shouted, "Let 'em through. Send the red one from earlier back here."

Six women emerged from two vehicles and walked towards the entrance. They were draped in full length coats and stilettos.

"Boy, dem hoes ain't playin'," Zeek said excitedly to Black Dave.

"They gotta be but bungie-ass naked up under dem jackets. Dat shit remind me of a movie I saw," responded Dave.

"I hope Rou let a nigga off dis door so a nigga can peep da action." Zeek held the door open, "What's up, ladies?"

"Nothing much, fellas." Poca pinched Zeek's face. "I hope y'all are not stuck out here and miss all the fun," she winked.

"I hope not my damn self," Rou said. Check him in his office," chided Black.

Poca turned around to the last girl, "Passion, why don't you keep these handsome guys company until we get ready to start," she smiled deviously and turned back to Dave and Zeek. "Y'all don't mind, do you?"

"Hell, nah; we don't mind," Dave smiled and rubbed his hands.

The rest of the pack entered the waiting area. L'il Bit, Spice, and two other girls went into the garage. Poca kept straight to Rouseau's office. The girls circled around the inside of the garage, prancing, making sure all attention was on them. Each girl posed in a corner of the garage, teasing with their facial expressions.

Pocahontas entered my office. I was on the phone. Buddha was sitting in a corner chair facing the door. She kept her eyes on mine the whole time while closing the door. Yeah, that's right show the boy respect. I got her.

"Well, damn you came prepared to work for real, huh?" I asked smoothly.

"Yeah, and I have a special treat for you. For looking out for us."

I looked at Buddha and smiled, turned back to face Poca, and nodded my head. That's what I'm talking 'bout – pay homage.

"I like surprises, especially when they look like you." She stood in front of the desk, spread her legs Wide, and fondled the belt on her coat.

Outside, Passion had Zeek and Black's imagination going with just her words.

"I'll give y'all a quick peep since y'all stuck out here. I feel sorry for y'all. Would you like that?" She stood in front of them. "And I won't even charge y'all."

"Would we like that? Do a chicken eat shit? Gotdamn right we wit' dat," Dave reached out to grab. She slapped his hand down.

"Uh-uh, have patience, baby. Good things come to those who wait." She grabbed the belt holding her coat together, untied it, and teasingly stuck one hand inside. She stuck her tongue out and licked slowly around her mouth, "Y'all ready?"

Inside the garage, L'il Bit "coincidentally" stopped in front of M1, who eased to the corner closest to the door when the girls came in; his designated corner. She backed up on him and started grinding. Spice and the other two girls happened to find three "strangers" in the other three corners of the garage to enchant. That took up the TV area, tonk tables, and pool tables.

All eyes were on them.

L'il Bit called out, "Y'all ready?" All da girls reached for their coat belts. They each grinded on their male counterparts while reaching inside their coats. By now everyone was rowdy and ready for the action. Money was shown everywhere. Their "coincidental strangers" were pretending to assist them in getting naked.

They rubbed their hands down the women's bodies and ended up in their coats. All the women opened their coats. M1, Chauncey, Goon, and Taterhead lifted Glocks out of the waistbands of the girls' attire and M1 said, "Any one of you horny-ass niggas move and your picture gonna end up on somebody t-shirt. Now everybody put they hands up."

Niggas went to grumblin' and mumblin', "What da fuck?"

"What da fuck it look like, nigga?" M1 said harshly. "Now you niggas can make it easy on yourselves, or you can make it hard. Everybody, back up to da walls. When my females tell you to come forward, dat's what you do." He turned to L'il Bit, "Pat and strip everybody down, four at a time, including shoes and socks. Put everything you find in this garbage bag." He handed her a Hefty. "Put all they clothes in a pile on the floor."

In one swift motion, Passion's hand came out holding a Beretta as her coat fell open. Zeek and Dave were shocked. They didn't know whether to watch the gun or watch her body.

"Good then. I guess a bitch don't have to tell you not to move. But if you do, I'll give you vasectomies that won't ever heal!"

"What, what's a vasectomy?" Zeek asked nervously.

She lowered the gun to his dick.

Poca's eyes turned cold and hard as she pulled the Glock from her waist-line and pointed at me. Then this bitch raised her eyebrow. My dick immediately got soft.

"Get your fuckin' hands in the air," she stated maliciously. I did so slowly, trying to get a grasp on the situation. Buddha started to reach for his pistol. She swung the pistol 'round to him and lifted her eyebrows.

"Go 'head, die for another nigga shit. You that stupid?" He reached for the ceiling. Soft-ass nigga. Do I know this hoe?

The door opened – "Poca".

The girls continued strip searching niggas, while the three young goons held everybody in check. Niggas was heated, but not stupid enough to try nothing with these young wild lookin' ass niggas!

M1 had gotten Zeek and Dave from outside, took their weapons, and threw them niggas in the garage with everyone else.

Poca didn't even turn around, "What up, cous'?" She said to M1.

"Just making sure you're okay," he said, as he walked over, patted Buddha, and confiscated his weapon. He pushed him on the floor facedown, hands behind his back, and walked behind the desk to me. "Alright, nigga, open da safe," he said calmly, "hold up – before you protest and lie," he looked me right in the eye, "If you don't, then I'll kill you," he assured me simply.

Who da fuck was this nigga? Where did he come from? All unanswered questions. Because I knew enough about him from his swagger to know he'd kill me.

I opened the safe.

———

SUNDAY, 3:45
CHILL

"Roll up, fool! I need to dull some of dis excitement I'm still feeling," M1 told me.

We were in the Leaf at one of his honeycomb hideout apartments.

"Hell, yeah, let's smoke one," jumped in Chaunce and Goon.

"I already got 'em rolled up. I figured y'all would need to mellow out. But y'all can take dat shit off y'all's faces now," I told 'em.

They had on actor's wax and fugazi mustaches, sideburns and other things to distort their features, courtesy of Poca. She was an aspiring actress with a membership to the SAG (Screen Actors Guild). She had access to all types of industry accessories.

"Shit, I'm a save mine. Matter of fact, give me all y'all's, too. We can use dis shit again." They headed to the bathroom, "I gotta ask Poca where we can get dis shit on our own," M1 yelled from da bathroom.

"Chill, you shoulda been there. We had all dem niggas butt-ass naked scareder than a mufucka!" Chaunce said excitedly when they returned.

"Yeah, fool, it was just like ol' times," M1 grabbed da joint from me.

I must admit, I did wish I was there. It was still in me, but I had to be smart. I had a lot more to lose now.

Knock, knock, knock.

M1 answered the door wit' his fire, while Chaunce stood in a dark corner with his.

"What took y'all so long?" M1 questioned Pocahontas as he let her, L'il Bit, and Spice in.

"You are so impatient. You told me to drop the other girls off at a new hotel and let Passion watch 'em. What up, Chill?"

"Ain't nothin', l'il momma. Heard dat shit was a cake walk."

"Dem flaw ass niggas," L'il bit said confidently.

"You still talking shit. I thought you was actin'. I guess not, huh?" teased Goon as the tension faded away.

"And I talk shit while I'm fuckin', too. And what!" Shot back L'il Bit.

"I bet I can make dat ass shut up!" Goon started boldly giving Chaunce dap.

"Young nigga, you still got milk round yo' mouth. You probably ain't even circumcised." Damn, she tried fool. Everyone cracked up on dat one.

That shut him up. Maybe he did have a pullback.

M1 and I broke off from everyone and left them in da living room while we went and counted the loot. We hit for $233,615. Not bad! We gave Poca, Spice, and L'il Bit fifteen stacks, Passion got ten stacks, and they other homegirls got five. We gave the l'il fools ten stacks a piece. That left us with sixty-nine thousand a piece. I felt well compensated.

This was the best sixty-nine that I'd ever been a part of! Sunday, 2:00 p.m.

"What dey do, fool? What's up Jr.?" I greeted them as they entered the Fun Zone. I was standing by the ball pit, watching DJ play.

Jap gave me dap, "What up, boy?"

"Hey, Uncle D," said an excited Jr., eyes already wandering, looking for DJ.

"Jr., Jr.!" DJ called out from inside the ball pit. "Jr., come on! Come get in with me!" He ran over to DJ.

"So what's new on yo' end?" I inquired.

"Same shit, different day. Ya know."

"Let's catch a table so we can chat." We sat down.

I passed him a shopping bag with ten stacks in it.

"What's dis, homebody?" He looked in the bag, sat Back, and looked at me, puzzled.

"What, you don't' want it?" I asked playfully.

"Fuck, yeah, I want it," he answered, with a big smile. I was just curious."

I took a sip of my coke and said, "We robbed yo' cousin last night," I said nonchalantly, and watched his reaction.

He looked skeptical, like, "Yeah, right." "Y'all robbed Rouseau?"

"Yeah, nigga. We touched Rouseau and the whole fuckin' gamblin' house. We hit 'em up last night, and, even though you wasn't a part of da shit, I'm just lookin' out, feel me? I know I don't have to tell you to keep it on da low."

"Bet dat up, fool. I appreciate it. I'm saying, you was there personally?"

"Nah, I wanted to be. But I know I had to be smart. So, nah, it was just M1 and da l'il goons out da Leaf."

"Damn, I knew you were a l'il sore at da nigga, but I ain't know you was thirty-eight hot."

I could tell he still had a lot of questions he wanted to ask, but I'd pretty much told him all I was gonna tell him. I only did that cause he was my right-hand man. Even so, I wasn't giving out all the details.

"Yeah, and now I feel better. Dat make up for some of dat cash he been making off our connect."

"I feel you. I feel you," he replied.

———

SUNDAY NIGHT
JAP

"Baby, why you so quiet?" asked Shay.

We were lying in the bed, watching TV. We had just finished making love, if you could call it that. It was more like grudge fucking.

"No reason, baby. I was just thinkin' 'bout something."

"What, how good your wife's pussy is?" she joked.

I smiled absentmindedly, "Yeah, dat too, baby."

She slapped my chest, "Stop lying, Jap. Tell me what you thinkin' about."

"You so nosy."

"No, I'm just inquisitive," she retorted.

"I was thinking about something Chill told me earlier."

"Uh oh, don't tell me he done messed around and caught AIDS, fucking all dem females."

"Do you always have to say dumb shit out yo' mouth? Dat's why I don't like to talk to you 'bout shit now. You so damn sarcastic!" I said heatedly. Niggas don't joke bout dat ninja (AIDS).

"I was just playing, Jap. Damn, I'm sorry. I was joking," she rubbed my chest. She tried to clean it up because she really was nosy and she'll say anything to find out what's on my chest.

But I really did want my wife's opinion.

"He told me some shit bout Rou today."

"Rouseau? Y'all back fooling around with him?"

"Nah, they robbed him last night."

"They robbed Rouseau? What you mean, they robbed Rouseau?"

"Just what I said. They robbed him at his car wash."

"So, why are you thinking about it so heavily? You feel sorry for him or something?"

"Hell, no. I was just wonderin' if it was da right thing to do. Wonderin' if it could tie back to Chill at all. We've come so far. I just don't want him to fuck it all up starting unnecessary problems."

"Well, baby, I don't know too much about robbing. But I do know that, even thought I don't too much like your homeboy, he is a smart muthafucker. I have to give him credit on that. So I don't think you should worry about anything, especially since you're not involved. You're not involved, right?"

"Dat's my nigga. If he's involved, then I'm automatically involved," I stared at her with a serious unit.

CHAPTER 13

CHILL
JUNE

The last couple of months had been alright. We'd been getting paperwork spo-
radically from different females that had jobs. We'd just save the paperwork
until we had two or three accounts to bust at one time, so we wouldn't waste
paperwork. It's Friday, June 5th. Lauren's birthday party is tomorrow. Let all
the working people get loose and rest on Sunday, if so inclined.

Let me call Jap and see what's up.

"What dey do, big homey?"

"Just getting a l'il shoppin' out da way. What's up?"

"Tryin' to see if you goin' to Lauren's party or if I'm flyin' solo?"

"Nigga, I been told you I was going! I gotta 'fit and all. Matter fact, I'm
gonna drop these groceries off, pick up Jr., and drop da fit off at yo' crib."

"So you ain't taking Shay, huh? I figured dat one. Dat's cool, ol' sneaky-ass
nigga. A real nigga would just put dat shit on at da crib and say fuck what wifey
say," I needled him.

"What da fuck eva! Things been tightwork (good) at da crib, so I'm tryin'
to keep it dat way as long as possible. I told her me and you was going to
Orlando on some business and we were leaving tomorrow evening. So I'm
good! We talked about her interruptin' business, especially after last time, so
she knows not to try dat no more. Shiit, I say da word 'business' or 'work' and
that shit gets me diplomatic immunity."

I laughed, "Whateva, dat shit sound good. It don't sound like pure freedom though. It sound like a ... weekend furlough."

"Dat's betta than nothin. It's betta than how she's been in da past."

"Yeah, especially for you. I guess you finally took off da skirt, but you still got on capri's!" I clowned my dawg. "And don't bother bringin' dat 'fit. You ain't been out in a while. Yo' swag outdated bout two years, fool. I'll get you right. You ain't finna embarrass me!"

"Fuck you, my nigga. I'll hit you up in a minute," he hung up.

———

We pulled up to Lauren's building. She stays in Coconut Grove, right on the bay. She had a plush penthouse suite. The night was very warm, but with a nice breeze off the water. Jap and I looked nice, in a laid back way, nothing too serious. We looked like two businessmen enjoying recreation. Me, I was fresh in a two-piece, beige linen, Roberto Cavalli summer suit with a cream, short-sleeved, Egyptian silk button-up and cream closed-in suede Bally sandals. Nothing major!

Jap was tightwork in a peanut butter two-piece made by Balenciaga. Underneath, he had on a soft yellow, short-sleeved button-up and peanut butter loafers – also by Balenciaga.

I had gotten Lauren a five-carat, champagne-colored, diamond tennis bracelet from Ross & Simon. After racking my brain, I figured I couldn't go wrong with diamonds.

The hired butler opened the door and let us in. We looked at each other like, "Wow!. This little shindig was on point!". I could tell Lauren's significant other put a lot into it. People were walking around serving hors d'oeuvres and champagne. She had a fully stocked bar and a quartet playing instruments.

"Mante, Jap, I'm glad you guys could make it," Lauren said. At the same time, she looked at me like, "Nigga, you better had come!"

"Of course, you both know Arthur, my boyfriend." Look at this cock sucka – up in her ass already!

"What's up, Art? Can I call you Art?" I extended my hand and looked him in the eye.

"I'm fine, and I'd prefer if you didn't call me Art," he said, as he returned the stare and gripped my hand tightly He didn't shake Jap's hand.

Lauren interrupted the tension, "Guys, make yourselves comfortable, and I'll introduce you to some of the other guests in a minute." She signaled a servant carrying champagne.

"Alright, thanks Lauren," Jap spoke for us.

They walked away.

The view was stunning. I admired her as she walked away. She was dressed in a seashell-colored backless form-fitting gown with thigh-high slits on both sides. I recognized it as a Nina Ricci design. The four-inch Dior open-mouthed heels had her calves looking well defined. The roundness of her ass, the spread of her hips, the arch of her bowlegs, and the beauty of her face, made her a femme fatale. The bulge in my pants reminded me of how thin my fabric was.

I had a funny feeling in my stomach. I guess some people would call it jealousy. I don't know 'cause I never experienced it before. Her boyfriend was more arrogant than me. He was the CEO of a company called Walkey International, a worldwide telecommunications company. They had been together for over a year.

Jap and I made our rounds and mingled for a bit. We ended up in a corner talking to the wives of two congressmen.

"So do you workout, Mr. Stevens?" Ida asked coquettishly. Ida Parcels was in her mid forties. She was about 5'7", slim figured, and brunette. She wore her hair in a bun, and a stylish mint-green Yves St. Laurent wrap skirt that showed off smooth tanned legs. Not bad looking – even had a little poot-booty. Too much makeup though! "Because I could use someone to help me with my squats," she rubbed a hand over her ass.

"I don't know, Ida, my workouts are pretty intense. It might be hard if you're a novice," I responded smoothly.

"I assure you, I am not anyone's novice. As a matter of fact, I could show you a new workout regimen or two!" Damn she's feisty!

"Well, in that case …" I started.

"Excuse us, Ida, Bev. I need to borrow these two for a minute. Please excuse us," interrupted Lauren.

"Oh! No problem, Lauren. These two make for delightful conversation," complimented Bev.

"Yes, they do," Ida winked at me, "I hope I can chat with you again before the night's over, Mr. Stevens."

"It would be a pleasure, Ida!" With that, Lauren pulled us away.

"Dam, dat was crazy. Fool, did you hear what dat lady said to me?" Jap asked me.

"No, I was having a very interesting chat with Mrs. Ida myself," I responded.

"Discussing workout routines with Ida, huh?" She looked at me and smirked.

"Yeah. How you know?" I asked curiously.

"Darling, Ida workouts with everybody, including women. Her and her husband are swingers," she looked at the expression on my face and laughed and goofy-ass Jap laughed with her.

"There goes my ego. I thought it was my suave demeanor and irresistible charm," I joked.

"Ooh, baby, you're irresistible to me," she pinched my cheek, "And that's all that matters. Come on let's meet some folk."

———

"Joshua Krimbel, I'd like you to meet a couple of friends of mine, D'mante Stevens and Japhier Poitier. Guys, this is Joshua Krimbel, the chairman of the Chamber of Commerce of Metro-Dade." We all shook hands.

"Pleased to meet you, Mr. Krimbel," I announced.

"Nonsense. The pleasure is mine. Please call me Joshua," he said with a broad smile. "What type of business are you into? Mr. Stevens and Mr. Poitier, correct?"

I did most of the talking because Jap wasn't used to these types of situations. See, I learned a long time ago; different people for different things. You can't treat everybody the same; therefore, you can't talk to everyone the same.

So I learned how to adapt and adjust to different people and situations. I was a chameleon. So right now I was in my sophisticated persona.

"Please, Mante and Jap would be fine, as that's what our friends call us. I'm the CEO of Diempur Corporation," I stopped to let Jap state his title.

"And I'm vice president of LEM Company," Jap cut in, smoothly following my lead.

"Both of which are midlevel companies specializing in import/export, mostly to third-world countries," I added.

"That's interesting."

"Joshua and his associates are looking for investors for a sort of renaissance renewal of the Overtown area of Miami," confided Lauren.

"Is that so? What a coincidence! Right, Jap?" He nodded. "We've been looking for some profitable investments around town," I stated.

"Well, look no further. I have a number of deals on the table, and I'm quite certain there's more than a few that you'd be interested in."

"I'll have my secretary schedule an appointment so we can…"

"That won't be necessary. Lauren has my personal numbers. Just give me a ring anytime."

"Right. Thanks. Well, it certainly was a pleasure." We all shook hands and then departed.

Jap left us to go talk to a couple of Miami Heat players who were in attendance. Sports and entertainment and he was right in his element. Probably 'cause he could still be hood.

"So where's your pit-bull of a boyfriend? He should be searching for you soon," I said sarcastically.

"Him and some of the fellas are in his office smoking cigars," she answered, while we headed to another group of people.

"I have something I want to give you for your birthday." I slipped my hand inside my pocket.

She stopped my hand and looked in my eyes, "Hold it. I want you to meet a couple more people and then you can give it to me," she smiled.

"Ah, Lauren, quite an affair you've put together, my dear," said a jovial Judge Denkins.

"Thank you, Judge. This is my close friend D'mante Stevens; and, D'mante, this is Judge Thomas Denkins and his wife Elizabeth."

We shook hands.

"Nice to meet you, Your Honor and Mrs. Denkins."

"Oh, please," he waved his hand, "Call me Thomas. I'll be Your Honor on Monday."

We chatted for a while.

"I have two more people I want you to meet. I believe you'll find use for them. I'll just introduce you to them. I don't want to know anything after that." She looked at me seriously. I was curious to know who this person was, especially after she provided a disclaimer.

We walked towards two women who were standing near the musical quartet, laughing and talking. One was toffee-colored with neatly wrapped shoulder length hair with a body built like a swimmer's. The other was a short, thick white woman with her skin so tanned it looked like she just stepped off the beaches of Jamaica. She had her hair cut in a boyish style. Judging by her back arms, she looked like she was no stranger to weights. And by the curve of her glutes, those squats were paying off. They looked to be in their thirties.

"Kathleen, Evelyn," they looked at Lauren as we stood in front of them, "I'd like you to meet a dear friend of mine, Ty'Quan Mitchell." My antenna went up immediately. She called out my nickname. That means she's hiding my identity from these ladies. Who the hell are they?

The two women appraised me from head to toe in a split second. They smiled, batted their eyes, and Kathleen, who was the white lady, spoke first, "Ooh, Lauren, where did you find this handsome stud?"

"Yeah, where you hiding him?" flirted Evelyn.

"Hi, ladies, pleased to make your acquaintance," I said, as I kissed their knuckles. Color flooded both their cheeks.

"Um, and a gentleman as well," chimed Kathleen.

I wish Jap was over here, but knowing him, he was probably talking to some producer, trying to get a record deal.

"TQ is a longtime friend of mine. He studies international finance," Lauren acknowledged.

"TQ, Evelyn is the branch manager for Nations Bank downtown, and Kathleen is the head teller," Lauren winked at me. Bingo! My mind is turning a thousand miles per hour. Now I understand the meaning behind her words.

"I see we have something in common, ladies," I slid in.

"Well, I'm glad it's money. I wonder what else we have in common," Kathleen stated rakishly.

It must be my cologne!

"Well, I'll leave you three to get better acquainted while I check on the other guests." Lauren walked off.

By the time Lauren came back, I had found out what I needed to know about Evelyn and Kathleen. Ev had been branch manager for about four years. She was thirty-five, unmarried, no kids, and open minded. Kathleen was her head teller and had been for three years. She was thirty-four with two kids and a sense of adventure. It won't take much to get them in action, especially since we have so much in common!

————

"Baby, it's beautiful. Oh, my God!" We were standing alone on the main balcony. I'd just given Lauren her birthday present. She hugged me and kissed me full on the lips.

I was reluctant to pull back.

"Girl, you better ease up. I don't wanna have to toss ya nigga off this balcony," I half-kidded.

"I'm just happy, Mante," she looked up and searched my eyes. "But what would really make me happy is you, baby." She grabbed my hand and turned me toward the balcony. It was a lovely sight overlooking the whole Biscayne Bay. She glided her hand slowly out across the scenery in front of us.

"Baby, the whole world is out there," she said in a low voice.

"Yeah, it's nice."

She turned my face toward her and placed my hand on her heart.

"Well, here is your world, in here, all to yourself."

"Um Um." Arthur appeared in the entrance of the balcony.

"Lauren, may I have a word with you?" It came out in a serious tone; more of a demand than a question.

She looked longingly in my eyes one last time, then turned and went to Arthur. He looked as if he wanted to kill me and eat me right there. I knew that I wouldn't be alone with her anymore tonight. I made one last circuit and went to find Jap.

CHAPTER 14

CHILL/JAP/SHAY
MONDAY, 7:22 P.M.

We were cruising through the city in Jap's F-350 Dually. I had just got through telling him about this feeling I had that, with Lauren's two friends on our team, shit was going to start poppin' off decent.

"So what you think?" he asked.

"Nigga, I just told you what I think!" I shot back.

"Nah, not dat."

"What you talking 'bout?"

"You think dem two broads fuckin'?"

I chuckled, "My nigga, I don't know. But one thing for certain, two things fa sho. You sure as hell won't find out."

"Why not?"

"Cause you married, and you life boring-ass shit," I laughed as I said, "The only threesome you gonna have is if Shay give you head, booty, and cock in one night," I cracked.

"Oh, you think you Don Juan and shit, huh?. I was gonna keep it on da low until I got da account, but I'm a have to show you what time it is right now, nigga!"

He called somebody on da phone.

"Hello, can I speak to Son'ye?" he asked.

"Who da fuck is Son'ye?" I thought.

"Dis Jap. Oh, what's up, Raven?. She in da tub? Yeah, dat's what I was calling for. I'm finna swerve thru there now. I'll be there in about twenty, thirty minutes." He listened and smiled, "Girl, you need to cut dat shit out. I'm gone."

Is dis nigga blushin'?

"Who dat was, fool?" I was curious as a muhfucka.

"Just two potential clients I snagged at da grocery store," he said smugly.

"Damn, so you snatchin' up females now? Welcome back from da dead, my nigga!" I said proudly. I was really shocked.

"Yeah, dawg, I know you been totin' da load wit' me and dis marriage shit. So a nigga just tryin' to do his part. You feel me?" He looked at me sincerely.

"I ain't sweatin' dat shit. You my nigga from da cradle to da grave. But fuck dat sentimental shit. What's up wit' dese l'il broads here?" I was anxious to see what kind of work my dawg up in since he been on hiatus for so long.

"You'll see. Just sit back and chill."

He cranked up da boom and flushed it up 27th Avenue towards Carol City.

———

Jap/15 minutes later...

<ring ring>

"Yeah, what's up, baby?" I answered for wifey.

"Baby, my taillight is out on my car, and I really need to take my mom to Wal-Mart. You know she likes to go at night." Shay pleaded, "Unless you want to take us!"

She thought she was slick. She was trying to see when I was coming home without asking me. Plus, she knew I didn't like her driving my Range. She thought that because it was a truck she could dog it out. She didn't understand that it was still delicate even though it was a SUV and that if you needed an ashtray for dat muhfucka they charge you a thousand dollars. But I was in a good mood. I looked over at my dawg in the passenger seat vibing. I was putting in work once again on my way to finesse a couple of bank accounts!

What da hell.

"Yeah, you can take the Range, baby. But do me a favor and drive my shit like you got some sense."

Pause. I know she was shocked.

"Uh, okay, baby. You're sure? Cause I could just wait on you." She tossed another hook in the water. "Yeah, right! Then when I get there, your mother 'mysteriously' changes her mind," I thought.

"Yeah, I'm sure, girl. I trust you and love you, too."

"Alright, love you," she hung up.

———

We were in Miramar, Broward County, just over the county line from Dade. A lot of rich white people and upper mid to rich blacks stayed in Miramar and the crackas was a bitch. These rednecks do not play. They response time was literally thirty seconds or less.

We pulled up to a nice brick house with a finely manicured yard with a couple of palm trees. It was an Acura and a Maxima in the yard. The front door opened and out stepped two of the baddest Spanish bitches I'd ever seen. Jap looked over at me, waiting for my reaction.

I gave my dawg a clap, "Yeah, boy, you did dat." I was secretly hoping that they'd give us a hard time with da accounts just so I'd have to fuck and suck it out of one or both of 'em. I didn't even wait for Jap. I jumped out and introduced myself.

"Buenas noches, sweetie," I called out.

"Tu habla Espanol?" the taller one asked.

"Nah, those are the only words, but I do speak in tongues," I said seductively as I reached the porch. They raised their eyebrows and giggled. Jap shook his head as well, and we all walked in the house.

I love this job.

———

Shay

"What's up, boo?" I asked my fuck buddy when he answered the phone.

"Nothin' much, girl. What's up with you?"

"Just took my mother to Wal-Mart and dropped her home."

"Long time no hear. I thought you ain't fuck with me no more."

"Boy, it's only been two weeks. Why, you miss me?" I teased.

"Yeah, I wanna suck dat fat pussy of yours. Where ya nigga at?"

My pussy just sprung a leak thinking about that boy tongue. He had a tongue so long it would make a rattlesnake jealous!

"He with his homeboy – supposed to be taking care of some business."

"So what dat mean? You got a l'il time to play?" he whispered seductively.

"I don't know. I don't know when he coming home, and I'm driving his car," I reasoned.

"Dam, that's fucked up. A nigga just wanted you to sit on my face for a l'il while," he enchanted freakily.

Um. Um. Um. My pussy is throbbing.

'Uhh, I probably can meet you for thirty minutes. You gonna stick a finger in my ass while you suck this pussy?" Damn, I'm horny.

"I was hoping you'd let me stick my tongue in there, too," he taunted me.

"Boy, where you at?" I was about to bite a hole in my bottom lip. You at home?"

"Nah, I'm at another l'il hideout I just copped. Write down the directions."

"Hold up, let me pull into this gas station." I swerved into Amoco. "Ok, let me find something to write with."

I looked in my purse. Shit, I got everything else but a pen. I checked the middle console; still no pen. Hold up! What's this?

"Hold on, boo. I'm coming."

Paper with a number on it. Son'ye. Who the fuck is Son'ye?

Well, let's find out. I found a pen in the glove.

"Give me the directions," I said, still thinking about the number. "I understand. I'll be there in twenty minutes."

In the meantime, let me see who Ms. Son'ye is!

"Hello, can I speak to Son'ye, please?" I asked politely.

"This is her. Who's calling?" she responded suspiciously.

"Hi, Son'ye. My name is Torie, and you don't know me, but I think you know my brother. At least, I hope you know my brother. His name is Jap.

"Yes, I know Jap."

"I'm calling you because... oh, my God, I can't believe this."

"Is everything ok?" asked a confused Son'ye.

"No, it's not! I have my brother's car, and it won't start. I can't get it to crank! I can't remember the last four digits to his cell phone! I found your number in the car, and I was hoping you knew the number! I don't know shit about cars, and I have my infant with me!" I pretended to cry.

Damn, I should win an award for this shit.

"Okay, calm down, don't panic. Everything's going to be fine. Are there lights around? And people? You're not on a dark street, are you?" she asked, concerned.

"I'm at a gas station on University Drive, but it's closed so there are no people round. I just want to get my baby home."

"Oh, well, that's not too far from where I stay. Jap just left here not too long ago. He can't be that far away. If you call him now, you can catch him before he gets too far. The number is 555-8728. Call him now. If you can't reach him, call me back, and I'll come myself, ok?"

This bitch ought to get a damn citizen's award with her friendly ass.

"Ooh, thank you sooo much. I really appreciate it. I was starting to panic." I feigned graciousness.

"Ahh, it's no problem. Bye."

I don't believe this shit. This nigga got the nerve to try me. Who the fuck do he think I am? I'll show him! L'Shay is the wrong bitch to fuck with.

"Hello?"

"I am not too far, so look out for me. I'm coming to get dat dick"

———

CHILL

"I gotta give you props on dat, fool. L'il momma and her homegirl was tight-work, boy!" I let him know.

"Yeah, nigga, just to let you know; don't put shit past a nigga," he retorted. "But, nah, I know you be toting most of the weight, my nigga. So I'm just tryin' to help out a bit. Ya feel me?"

"Yeah, I feel you, my nigga. But I ain't sweatin' dat shit. We gettin' money, fool, and…"

<Ring ring ring> JAP

"Dis Son'ye right here, fool. I guess I got my swagger back," I joked.

"What dey do, mommy?" I answered.

"Hey poppy. I'm just calling to make sure your sister got in touch with you," she inquired.

"My sister?" I curiously looked at Chill.

"Yeah, she called me because your car broke down on her, and she's stranded with her baby. She didn't reach you yet?""

Ah, shit. I done fucked up somewhere.

"Nah, but I'm finna call her right now. It's probably just the kill switch on the car. Let me check it out. I'll hit you back."

"Ok, poppy."

She hung up.

I looked over at Chill. "My nigga, I think I done fucked some shit up," I admitted nervously.

"What happened? What she talkin' bout your sista?" You ain't even got a sister."

I was thinking fast, "Damn, I must've…I had to…I thought I threw dat shit away."

"Damn dawg, what you talkin' bout?" He asked anxiously.

"Man, Shay called…I mean it had to be Shay who called Son'ye and said she was my sister and she was stranded in my car."

"What? I'm sayin', how she got da number?"

I took a deep breath and exhaled, "I had to leave it in da whip. I meant to…I actually thought I tossed it out. I guess it slipped my mind. I been drivin' dis shit since I went to the grocery store dat day. Fuck?"

He looked over at me like he was disappointed in me. "Yeah, you slipped, fool. But rule number 1: don't panic. Call Shay, tell her what time it is. She gonna be .38. Well, shit, she already hot, but still be honest. It ain't like you fuckin somethin'," he advised.

I called her phone about ten times; no answer. I swung by my crib; not home. Then I went to her mother's and finally by Trenice crib. Ain't nobody saw her.

Dejected and worried, I took Chill to his crib.

"Just holla if you need me, fool. You might as well go home and wait. Jr. is at her niece house for the whole week since school out, right?"

"Yeah, why?"

"Cause you gonna need some private time to beg!" With that, he jumped out.

"Yeah, I know," I said to myself, and pulled off.

————

SHAY

"I'm a hurt that dick. Ooh, gimme that dick. Yeah...mmm...mmm...just...like...dat...ummm fuck... harder."

"Take dat dick, bitch," he growled as he slapped my ass while fucking me from the back. My pussy spasmed as another nut ripped through my body.

Afterwards, we lay exhausted like we ran the NY marathon. I didn't even care about the time. Fuck the time! My fuck buddy dozed off. I smiled. I put it on his ass! I'm a savage in bed when I'm angry.

I got dressed and left. I didn't bother waking him up. When I got in my car, I check my phone. I had twenty missed calls from Mr. Jap. Fuck him!

————

JAP

I heard da door open around two in da morning. I watched Shay toss her handbag on the table. I had been sitting in the living room since I came home. I was ready to get this over with.

"Where you been?" I asked, 'cause I didn't know what else to say.

"I've been out thinking about what a fool I've been. Besides, shouldn't you be asking Son'ye where she's been, not me?" Her words were calm and bitter.

"There you go, jumping to conclusions. Son'ye is just a potential client for business."

"Fuck business. I don't want to hear that shit. As friendly as that girl was to me, I know you're fucking her. But that's ok, though. You ain't got to worry about *ever* fucking me, period!"

"What dat supposed to mean?"

"What part don't you understand? I'm not fucking your dirty dick ass!"

"Son - I...I mean, Shay, I --"

"Nigga, what you just call me? You just called me dat bitch name. Get the fuck out my face!" she yelled, walked down the hallway to the bedroom, and closed and locked the door.

I stretched out on the couch and wondered, "Could I be any stupider?". What type of nigga leave phone numbers around for his girl to find? A dumb-ass nigga, that's who. I'll let her sleep on it. Hopefully, shit be straight in da morning. Hopefully.

SHAY
In the shower

I can't believe he called me her name. That's okay, whatever he can do, I can do better. I won't give him the satisfaction of fucking her and me! I wonder how many others there are. Just like my father; I knew I was right. It was only a matter of time before I found out. I should've questioned her. I should've asked her how many times they fucked. Fuck that! That bitch would've lied anyway. I wonder what she looks like. I wonder how he fucked her. Did she ride his dick? Did he fuck her from the back? Did he eat her pussy?

Ahhhhhhhhh!

What am I doing? Why do I feel this way? Why am I in the shower stroking myself, thinking about my husband with another woman? Am I some kind of pervert?

Did he fuck her bare?

Did she cum on him?

My body shuddered as my pussy pushed its juices out into the tub and down the drain.

———

JAP

My back is sore as hell from sleeping on da couch. I hope Shay comes out da room so I can straighten out dis mess I created.

I fixed me a bowl of oatmeal and waited. It was seven a.m. I know she had to be to work at 8:30.

7:20 – fuck it. I can't wait no longer. I got up and knocked on da bedroom door.

"What?" she screamed.

"Man, I need to get in da room and get dressed, too," I lied. "Plus, I need to holla you and straighten dis shit out. You goin' overboard."

"Fuck you! Do you think I'm stupid, nigga?"

"If you listen to me, I can explain, instead of yelling through the door."

Silence.

"What? What can you possibly have to say to me?" she asked in a stubborn tone.

"Listen, I met her at Winn Dixie when I went shopping Friday. She was in front of me in line and paid for her groceries with a debit card. I saw that and started thinking about how Chill has been totin' all da weight. So I hollered at her to get her bank account. That's it. I talked to her a few times to butter her up, and den I brought Chill in last night to finish it off."

"You thought about how Chill be toting all the weight? Nah, nigga. What you meant to say was you thought about how Chill be having all the fun. What, you bored with our marriage? You feel like you missing something? You think…"

"Man, it ain't even like that. I'm tryin' to take care of us, my nigga."

"And you hollering at hoes is more important than making your family comfortable?"

"Stop putting words in my mouth. You wanna see shit your way, but when you spending a nigga chips, shits okay! You want the luxuries of havin' cash, but you don't wanna let me do what's necessary to get it. You can't have it both ways!"

"Fuck you, Jap! You just want an excuse to be hoeish. You ain't got to holla at no hoes to get money. How many times you been to her house? How much more weight have you taken off Chill's shoulder?

"Dat's da first girl I hollered at since I told you I'd quit over a year and a half ago."

"Whatever! How many times you been to her house, Jap? Answer that one."

"I went to her house twice. Last night was the third time with Chill," I admitted.

"And you're not fucking her? Nigga, please! You fucked her. That's why she was so friendly to me when she thought I was your sister. Boy, I'm not stupid by a long shot."

"Man, I…"

"That's ok, 'cause I bet you won't be puttin' no dick in this pussy. I should divorce your ass!"

"So what you saying, Shay?"

"What you don't understand, nigga? You smart, ain't you? Figure it the fuck out!"

CHAPTER 15

CHILL

"Ladies," I said as I stood to greet Evelyn and Kathleen. We were meeting for lunch at Pietro's, an outdoor restaurant on swanky South Beach, known for their Mussels Marinara. "I'm so glad that you could make it."

"Ty'Quan, we wouldn't have missed this meeting of the minds for the world," said a jovial Evelyn.

"Hmm, the two M's, money and men," Kathleen seconded.

I signaled the waiter. It was a beautiful day; eighty degrees, sunny, with a delicate breeze directly off of the ocean, which was less than a hundred feet away.

"I'll have a Mojito," ordered Kathleen.

"And I would like a Mai Tai and an order of raw oysters," Evelyn put in.

We made small talk until the waiter came back with their drinks and oysters.

"So, how are you two feeling about what we discussed?" I inquired.

"Everything sounds okay. We've been thinking a lot about your proposition, weighing the pros and cons, and we're leaning towards accepting," answered Kathleen.

"I mean, basically, we want to talk numbers and details," added Evelyn.

"Well, the way I have it mapped out is that, since you're the branch manager, I'd send the clients to you in order for you to open the accounts. Now, when the clients come to you, they'll be fully equipped with two forms of ID, a state, and a credit or debit card in the name of the ID. They'll have the Social either memorized or written somewhere inconspicuous. All of which are fake, but will meet the bank's criteria, credit wise, and also they won't be the Telecheck system."

"Sounds very well thought out. You have your bases covered on the initial startup. That's great, because if all of our clients' info is up to par, then they appear as regular customers. That shouldn't raise any red flags on my end. It's two others that's allowed to open accounts. I could also use their codes for the computer to throw it off even more," Evelyn informed me.

"Great," I said, which it was. Anything done by a person in a bank, by computer, required that or someone's code. That way if it's any mistakes or any fraudulent activity, the bank knows who, what, when, where, why, and how.

"One more thing… Your other job would be to keep us supplied with copies of different companies' payroll checks. As manager, I take it you get to work thirty minutes to an hour before everyone else?"

"Yes, that's true, if Kathleen doesn't ride with me. Still, she's usually the first one after me to arrive. What kind of payroll checks are you looking for? Anything in particular?"

"Obviously we wouldn't want fast food, grocery stores, or small retail places. I mean anything that we couldn't explain an employee getting an eight or nine thousand dollar check is out the question. I'm sure you have some in mind, Kathleen. As head teller, I'm sure you have some companies memorized that fall within our parameters. If not, then over the next month, just take a mental inventory of what companies pay out the heftiest sums. If possible, keep tabs on payment schedules also. That gives me an idea of when a company usually does its accounting," I explained.

"You want, basically, any place where salaries can be flexible, where the salaries are flexible, where there's no way to tell minimum from max."

"Right. Now, on your end, Kathleen, all you have to do is make sure the checks don't incur any holds once they're deposited. Make sure the next day, which is your bank's policy, as long as the account is in order and nothing is suspicious."

"I mean, they wouldn't have to actually come to you to deposit, but if another teller asks you whether to hold or to clear, you recommend clear. We just need to make sure the pickup of the funds goes smooth once they come to make a withdrawal, which, knowing you all get there first, we'll send them early in the morning so they could possibly get to you.

"Your job is the biggest risk. Cause I know on deposits and withdrawals, it's your code in the computer. But you have a safety net in the fact that none of the clients know you. Plus, the way I'm going to run it down, they won't know you're involved. And number two, everything about our clients is fake. So the investigators will run into dead ends. So they can suspect, but they can't convict. Everything would be circumstantial. Worst come to worst, you be simply fired. If they do that wrong, you'd have a suit on your hands for wrongful termination." I sat back and looked in each one of their eyes trying to read their inner selves.

Nobody said anything for a minute as everything marinated. This was the beginning or the end for our little friendship.

Finally Kathleen nodded her head, "Well, from the gist of what I'm hearing, I like it. I do understand the risks. Since I wasn't planning on staying past the beginning of the year, that makes things even more attractive. I just want the worst-case scenario to be the potential of being fired. I can deal with that," she assured.

"Everything is a go on our end, Ty'Quan. We'll probably do a little fine-tuning to the plan amongst ourselves, but only to ensure our safety. But the overall plan is extremely well thought out. You know a lot about banks. I'm impressed. And even though I would like to avoid it, if it's worth my while, I can even stand being fired. So, next on the agenda: what's the split?" questioned Evelyn.

"Four ways: Me, you two, and Jap. Everyone gets twenty-five percent. We pay our clients, or should I say, employees together. Jap and I will incur the cost of the IDs, debits or credits, and Socials. Someone owes us a favor, so it shouldn't matter much. What do you think?"

"I'm thinking that's exactly what we were thinking for our risk and part in the scheme of things. But we know you guys have to get the girls, identities, and monitor things. We thought you would've said sixty/forty your way, which we would've accepted, but we underestimated you," admitted Evelyn.

"Sixty/forty would've had you satisfied, but I'm about making my partners happy. It keeps the hostility and envy down. I understand the risks and the value of your livelihoods more than you think. Plus, I want the understanding that we're more than just involved in this venture together. We're family, and I want us to stick together – period. We can't ignore the fact that jail could be in the picture for any one of us, right?"

"Yeah, you're correct, and we've considered it. And I believe I can safely speak for both of us when I say that as long as you're honest and fair with us, on our mothers' lives, you don't have to worry about us backstabbing and/or tattle-telling on you. I know you think we're green and we can't hold our weight, but we believe in loyalty a lot, a whole lot. Even if it means sacrificing ourselves, as long as it's a two-way street," explained Evelyn passionately.

I pondered.

"Well, I know you say you're speaking for both of you, but I would feel more confident if I heard it out of your mouth too, Kathleen."

"You have it right now, on my life. I give you my complete loyalty," assured Kathleen.

I smiled.

"Ladies, I couldn't have said it better myself. But one thing, I'm trying to be more than honest and fair with you. I'm trying to make you both millionaires!"

We all smiled and tasted what was left of our drinks. With that, we shook on the deal and enjoyed each other's company.

Later on I would put contingencies in place for Jap and I.

Promises are meant to be broken, and I had little doubt that theirs would be if the police or the Feds stepped down on them.

CHAPTER 16

CHILL

"What dey do, fool?" I asked my dawg. I was in a good mood, happy dat everything was going according to plan.

"Ain't nothin', my nigga. What up?"

"I met up wit' Evelyn and Kat yesterday. Everything is a go. We just need to make sure our end is straight."

"Yeah! They went for everything?" He was happy. "Damn boy, it's about time we got an inside connect."

"I broke it down to 'em. I gave it to 'em raw and uncut, no game. Alright, eighty-five percent raw and uncut. I put a lil l'il somethin' on it."

"So what does yo' gut tell you about dose two?"

"My gut tells me dat as long as everything goes well, we'll have a very successful partnership. Shit get a l'il sticky, well, dat could be a different story."

"I dig it. Still, dis is da best news I heard in two weeks. Shit been crazy on my end."

"So, I guess dat mean Shay still ain't given you no ass."

"Ain't no dope, my nigga. I'm still in da doghouse. I've tried every tactic known to mankind: flowers, singin' telegrams, begging, everything, my nigga!"

I could hear da frustration in his voice. So I tried to lighten my homeboy mood.

"Let me find out you on da street in da free world, jackin' ya dick!"

Silence.

"Aw, nigga. Gotdamn, fool. Go get you some pussy somewhere else or at least some head. Man, you trippin'."

"If I did dat, it'll only make shit worse, not better. I just have to be patient and weather the storm. She'll come around."

"Sometimes, my nigga, you sound flaw as fuck."

"Yeah, I feel you. But, sometime you gotta man up. G-shit, dawg."

"What you mean?"

"Dawg, you know I don't get in ya marriage game room, it ain't my place. But in dis case, I'd be dead wrong not to offer you some jewels of knowledge."

"I'm listenin'. I could use all da advice I can get."

"Number one, don't beg, don't ask. Matter of fact, don't even hint that you want some pussy. Every time you do, you give her more power. Go about ya business like everything is copacetic. Don't treat her nasty, don't have an attitude, just do you, ya dig? You gots to know dat females get horny just like a nigga do. But they like the power of holding pussy over a nigga head cause niggas let 'em. In da scheme of things, dick is just as precious a commodity as gold, diamonds, and pussy. Speaking common sense, dick sell just like pussy sell, ya dig?"

"Aight, aight! I feel you, my nigga. I gotta suck it up and be strong?"

"Yes, but you gotta use what you got, just like she is. Now let's take it a step further. What's her sign?"

"You know she's an Aquarius. Why?"

"Ok, I'm an Aquarius, my nigga. We have very high libidos..."

"Libi- what? What da fuck is dat?"

"Libido, silly nigga! Damn, you don't read? Ya sex drive."

"Oh. Well, shit, why you ain't just say sex drive, nigga?"

"My bad for thinkin' highly of you. I'll put you on da short bus now," I laughed.

"Fuck you."

"Anyway, listen. Aquarians have very high sex drives and we're freaky as fuck. So peep game. I'll bet you she fingerin' herself just as much as you gunnin'. So now take ya showers when both of y'all in da bedroom. When you come out, come out naked. Stroke up a l'il in da bathroom, come out, let her see ya meat hang. Tease and tantalize, my nigga. When you workout, do it when she at home. Come in da house, no shirt, swoll up and sweatin', ya feel me?"

"Yeah, yeah, I like dat. I like dat."

"Finally, pay a couple of females dat stay in yo complex to speak to you seductively, in a flirtatious way, while you and Shay either comin' or going. Act like you don't even notice da way dey speak or look at you. I bet Shay will notice even if you just pay a girl to look at you like she sweatin' you. Women always do. It'll make her more protective of you. Most of all, it'll make her appreciate more what she has. She'll see dat other women dig you, she'll do whateva to keep or get you attention. Basic laws of attraction, my nigga!"

"I'm feelin' all that shit! This is what I'm talkin' 'bout, homeboy. I'm gonna show her two can play her game. I been goin' bout dis shit da wrong way. It's time to switch up da game plan."

"Just be cool, keep a level head, and be patient. Dat's da sort of mannin' up I'm talkin' 'bout."

"Bet dat up fool. You're a real nigga. I felt a l'il trapped, but now I feel like I got some options."

"Fa sho. So I'm finna work on dis money plan and work dis shit thoroughly on my chalkboard. Be easy, I'll holla later."

"Aight. We'll meet up tomorrow. I'll pull out my chalkboard tonight too. I'll holla."

"Yo."

I ended da phone call. I didn't tell him the other thing about Aquarians is that we're hoeish. We love to experiment and try different shit. I wouldn't ever say it to him unless I had proof. But I been had da feelin' dat Shay was loose. It'll all come out, too! Dat's fa damn sho.

CHAPTER 17

M1

I was in Cloverleaf in one of my l'il honeycombs I used to put dat sac(drugs to be sold) on da block. I been sitting here watchin' dis muhfuckin' video and I still can't believe da shit I'm seein'. Eitha dis nigga must be death struck or he got to be da dumbest nigga in all civilization. At first, I though my mind was playin' tricks on me, maybe I had too much going on and I was slippin'. But two weeks ago, I hit da Spy Shop and got me a l'il somethin' just in case. Now I had all da evidence a nigga needed.

"Hey Goon," I called in to da walkie talkie watch I was wearin'. Everyone was out and about in da trap.

"What up, One?" he hit back.

"Hey, snatch up Chaunce and y'all come holla at me."

"Fa sho!"

Ten minutes later

"What dey do, bossman," greeted Chaunce.

"Y'all niggas sit down. I wanna show y'all somethin'. I'm showin' y'all dis cause ova da last couple week y'all reassured me dat y'all was G-code. Y'all been wit' a nigga da longest, but you neva know, but I see y'all one hundred so peep dis shit."

They looked at each other, confused and curious.

"Man, you a nig…" Chaunce started, but I cut it off wit' my hand.

"Remember, I told y'all a couple weeks ago dat dis apartment looked too plain, dat it look like somethin' going on in here. I told y'all I was finna jazz it up a l'il bit."

"Yeah. Then you went and bought them pictures and plants. It do look like a bitch live here," responded Goon.

"Y'all see dat picture right dere? Da big one wit' da African people on it?" I asked.

Dey both looked up and nodded.

"Well, my nigga, dat ain't no picture. Well, it is a picture, but da frame is a camera."

I looked at them. I could see da wheels turnin' in their head. They both know they ain't do nothin' wrong, but they knew somebody fucked up.

"Y'all see dat smoke detector in da kitchen? I took da real one out and replaced it wit' a camera too."

Both of their mouths dropped.

"Close ya mouths for somethin' fly in it." I hit play on da video. Y'all check dis shit out."

As we sat back and watched da footage their expressions went from surprised, to confused, and then angry.

"Dat pus-ass nigga," cried out Chaunce.

"You want me to handle dat nigga?" questioned Goon. "Man, why you ain't been tell us so we coulda been split his whole kool aid pack?"

"I had to make sure y'all wasn't part of da play. Dat's why I said I know y'all loyal. Y'all are on da video just as much as him, just different shifts. Now we gonna handle dat together, feel me?"

"Fo sho, my nigga," Goon backed up.

"Damn skippy," Chaunce added.

———

"Hey you boy, ain't no use for all that gruntin' and cryin'. Dat shit ain't gonna save you, nigga," I assured Taterhead.

We were on da way up I-75 headed towards Naples where it turned into Alligator Alley. They called it dat for a reason. I had my righthand bitch, Porsche, drivin' wit' Goon and Chaunce taggin' along. We were in a tinted out Eddie Bauer Expedition, wit' Taterhead tied and gagged in da third row. He was da source of all da noise. We waited until he came on shift at midnight and told him we was finna go step down on some niggas, just to get him in da truck. Now besides being hogtied, he was in a whole lotta pain. I had da blood on da plastic lining to prove it.

But it'll be over soon.

"Pull ova right here, Porsche."

We was dressed in all-black with black boots. We had night vision, pistols, gauges, and a l'il somethin' special. I had another vehicle parked about a mile behind us wit' "car trouble," to let us know if and when any police or otha funny lookin' vehicles were headed our way.

"Damn, One, it's darker than a bitch out here," stated a nervous Chauncey.

"Dis shit look scary out here, just like some shit a cracka would walk through, curious and shit, and get killed," joked a calmer Goon.

"Y'all two grab dat nigga out da back. I'll grab da supplies."

Taterhead was twitchin' and growlin' through da bind. I checked da bind. I checked da walkie talkie.

"All clear?" I asked.

"All clear," I got in response.

"Let's move out. Everybody put ya goggles on."

We started walkin' towards da forest line. On dis stretch of highway, it was no exits, no lights, and no help. It was pitch black wit' trees and bush on both sides. Furtha down, in da woods, were ponds and lakes and where nothin' lived, nothin' but gators. We had night vision goggles and a sawed off, plus our regular straps. In case we met some before we dropped his ass off. Fa sho, it's easier ways to kill a nigga, but I'm all about makin' an impression. I can be a sadistic-ass nigga!

"Right here, my nigga." We had walked about forty, fifty yards inside da forest. I picked a spot dat looked halfway between da nearest pond and da tree line. Right in da middle of some high ass brush and grass. We all looked around slowly through da goggles. You could hear da gutter sounds of da gators all around us.

"Nigga, you nervous?" I asked Chaunce.

"Hell yeah, my nigga. I'm scared than a muhfucka. I can deal wit' a hundred niggas, but dis nature shit is different," he responded.

"Relax, dey our friends. Take dat nigga clothes off," I demanded.

"Hand me da bleach, One. I'll bury dese shits," Goon said.

Plan was to dig a small foothole, stick da clothes in, pour bleach on 'em for DNA, if dey eva get found, and cover da hole.

I slapped Taterhead wit' da butt of da gun.

"Shut da fuck up fo' you wake up my friends," I started laughing. You betta be real still you'll last longer."

"Let me do da blood," pleaded Chaunce.

He proceeded to drench Taterhead's entire body in fresh chicken blood.

"Ummmmmmmmmmmmm, uhhhhhhhh," he growled.

"Bitch, shut up!" hollered Goon.

"Man up, nigga," added Chaunce.

I kneeled in front of Taterhead face.

"Was it really worth it? Was fifty measly ass grand really worth you life, Nigga?" I asked him. "Think about dat and let me know whenever I join you in hell, fuck nigga." I spit in his face.

We walked off.

———

15 minutes later

"Right ova dere, Henry," Bubba shined his flashlight through the brush. The reflection from the light caused the gator's eyes to glow red. "We got us a biggun!"

Henry and Bubba were out poachin' gators. Most gator poachin' is done at night to avoid the FWC (Florida Wildlife Commission). You could make a killing with gator skins.

"We got's da follow it, Henry. Watch ya step, Henry."

"You betcha, I..."

"Shh. He's on da move. I reckon he a twenty-footer. Dat's alotta skin, Henry."

Ummm. Ummm. Ummm.

"You hear dat, Bubba? What's dat?"

"Shut up, Henry! Before he hear us," Bubba chastised Henry. "Get da stun stick ready, Henry, she movin' faster."

"Im ready, Bubba, I'm ready!" cried out Henry.

"A little closa, Henry. Remember right through the head." They paced off the last few steps. "Now, Henry, now"

Boom.

"I got 'em, Bubba. I got 'em."

174

"Hit 'em again, Henry, to make sure."

Boom.

Bubba patted Henry on the back. "Good fuckin' shot, Henry. Right through da head."

Ummm. Ummm.

"We'd get pl –"

"Ssh. I heard somethin'."

"But, Bubba, I told you bef –"

"Shut up, Henry. Dere it is again." They both cocked their heads and listened. "It's comin' from ova dere."

They eased about fifteen feet in the direction the gator was headed.

"What the he –"

Umm. Umm. Umm. Umm.

"What a we got 'ere, Henry?" Bubba asked, as he shined the light down on Taterhead. "Look like a naked nigger."

"And he got blood all over 'em, Bubba."

"I reckon we us some gator bait." He looked down into Taterhead's eyes. "Ain't dat dere, boy."

He took the gag out of Taterhead's mouth.

"Please, please, y'all have to help. Dey tried to kill me, please."

"Now just a second dere, boy. I ain't seen a nigger alive worth my help. Seem like I'd be wastin' good gator bait in your case. You just helped me and

Henry catch dat twenty-foota ova yonder. I reckon ten, twenty more seconds and you'd be Kibbles 'N Bits."

"Look, look, just listen. I –"

"I ain't listen ta no dark skins."

"Wait. I –"

"Henry, we got us some live gator bait. Yesiree bob, dis 'ere is better dan usin' stray dog." Bubba proudly acknowledged.

"Money. I got money," pleaded Taterhead.

"What you say dere, boy?" Bubba ears perked up.

"I got money."

"It look to me you ain't gotta damn thing dere, boy."

"I can have my girlfriend bring it to you."

"How much money we talkin' about?" questioned Bubba.

"Ten thousand cash!"

"Oooooh weeee," cried out Henry.

"You hear dat, Henry? We don't hafta sell no gator skins for a while."

"Yeah, I hear, Bubba. Loud and clear."

"Where you gonna get all dat money from dere, boy?" You some kind of rich nigga?" Bubba asked.

"She'll bring da money. You can hold me 'til she get here." Taterhead's mind was thinking fast.

"Well, I reckon if you can get ten you can get twenty. What you think about dat, Henry?" He asked as he looked up at his cousin.

"I reckon so, Bubba."

"Yeah, yeah, I'll get da twenty!"

"Now you wouldn't be playin' now, would ya, boy?" Bubba bent down and peered closer into his eyes.

"No! Please, just don't leave me out here!"

"Henry, untie 'em." Bubba stood back with the shotgun. "You try something stupid, boy, and you'll be one dead nigger."

Henry untied him and stood him up.

"Hey, Bubba, what we gonna do with dat dere gator?"

"Ah, screw dat gator. We got us a nigger."

Bubba and Henry stalked off with their prey.

CHAPTER 18

The game has changed for the better. We now no longer have to search for women with ready accounts. Now we could almost use any female, almost. It was also easy to use friends and family, but worse come to worse, those people know you. So over the last few weeks, I've debated and debated. I've still been in the streets vibing up chicks, but I came to a conclusion I should've in the first place.

I'm going to use Pocahontas and her whole squad!

Think about it. Not only does that give us at least five girls, off bat, but with a little spirit gum, makeup and the whole nine on the disguises, those ten girls become twenty. I could open up, at the very least, two accounts in each girl's name.

It's time to get things poppin'. The accounts have to sit at least thirty days to mature. Most banks have a thirty-day new account policy in which new accounts are under heavy scrutiny for that time period. It's now Saturday, June 27th. I want to be up and running by the second week in August, at the latest.

It's time to get to work.

"What's up, M'bouli?" I asked as he answered. He was a west African friend of mine. I met him through M1, when he was copping weight from One. He'd gotten into some shit and wound up getting deported last year. While he was away, I looked out for his wife and daughter. He's been back about a month and already ws up and running.

"How it go, Chill?" You ready to get a move on it? Last time we talked, you say you go call back when ready. Everything on me end is in place."

"Yeah, I'm ready to start my summer gardening. How much you charging for your native handmade flower pots?"

"I have nutting but love for you, bretren. How many flower pots do you need?"

"Well, I'm trying to raise a new breed of lilies. So I was thinking maybe twenty to start out."

"Me normal price would be sixty dollars for my pots at three dollars a pot. But fa you, I give you all twenty fa say twenty-five dollars. How is dat?"

"Dat's love. I appreciate dat. I got you on da back end."

"You good, bretren. You took care of me family. For dat, me always indebted to you. Let's say you come tru Monday. Good?"

"Yeah, dat's tightwork. I'll holla then."

That was a good lookout on Bouli's behalf, from sixty thousand to twenty-five thousand, for twenty packages, including Social Security cards, identification, and credit card to match. Now I just need to get Poca and everyone else in place. They'll have to drive down from ATL tonight. I got 'em on standby, so it shouldn't be a problem.

———

We've been hard at work all week. The girls got in town late Sunday night. First, we used a real estate friend of Lauren's to get a six-month lease on an already furnished, five-bedroom hideout for the girls. I want them to have enough space to be comfortable and set up a decent makeup and disguise room. I don't wanna leave any trails at hotels.

Monday, Jap and I had a long detailed meeting with all of them. We laid everything out in a professional manner. Poca, Spice, L'il Bit, Passion, Mya, and Heaven knew us very well or were at least familiar with us. But in the latter two cases, we wanted everyone on the same page. We wanted everyone to know it was business before bullshit.

Afterwards, we split into two groups. Jap and I each took five women. Me and the first group went out and met up with Bouli at his studio. After the meeting, Jap and the second group went in the afternoon.

Tuesday, we repeated the same routine. Only difference was, this time all the girls were in their fake personas. The packages were ready for pickup early Thursday before sunrise. We spent the whole day scattered out, going from bank to bank, using branch location brochures from the customer info desk, opening up accounts. Jap and I basically hit the same banks at different times.

I'd changed my mind about strictly using Evelyn for the open-up procedure. The ID packages were just that good, so we used different banks. In the end, we had twenty brand new checking accounts. I made sure to keep hold of all the ID packages. Don't need no one trying no slick shit.

As of today, Friday evening, everything is in order and going as planned. I've been in touch with Kathleen and Evelyn. So far, they provided me with five different company checks. That's a good start. Hopefully, by the time we crank up next month, we'll have at least ten. Tomorrow is the 4th of July. Since we worked all week, I decided to show the girls a good time and have a cookout tomorrow. Just so everyone could unwind and relax.

CHAPTER 19

FRIDAY NIGHT
SHAY

I haven't had sex with my husband in just about a month. Thank God for my fuck buddy! Or else I would've been jumped on him, especially the way he looks when he gets out the shower. My husband is no slouch at 6'2, 220 and brown skin. His body is not super-defined, but it's chunky and solid. The way he walks out the bedroom with his dick swinging gets my blood boiling, and that's when I call F.B. By the time his punishment is over, Jap is gonna had learned a valuable lesson. I'm to be respected and appreciated at all costs!

Although, lately, he hasn't been pressuring me about sex. He's been very patient. That could only mean one of two things: either he's trying to be understanding or Sonye or some other bitch is breaking him off. And I don't believe any man to be that patient. Every time that thought crosses my mind, it makes me want to work harder to come out on top.

"Hey, baby," he greeted me as he walked in the bedroom.

"You just came from working out?," I could tell 'cause he was sweaty and bulging with no shirt on. His musty scent was turning me on.

Bastard!

"Yeah, I ain't do too much though. Just a lil' something to work up a sweat. How ya day was?"

"My day was okay. What about you, what did you do today?"

"Take care of business, runnin' all cross town from home to Ft. Lauderdale. Where's Jr.? At ya ol' girl house?"

"Yeah, she wanted him early tonight, so I took him. So what was in Ft. Lauderdale?" I questioned.

"We had dem females we had to take from bank to bank and open accounts. I explained dis shit to you already," he said, annoyed.

"Yeah, but you said it was eight or ten girls. How y'all managed that?"

"I took half, he took half."

"So you were riding around by yourself with five bitches all day?" I don't think I liked that.

"Yeah, what's ya point?" he stopped looking in the drawer, turned, and looked at me.

"I'm just asking."

"Don't start dat shit. I'm too tired. You'll be talking to youself!"

Or my fuck buddy!...I thought to myself.

"What you doin' tomorrow?" he asked, bringing me out of my thoughts.

"Go early in the morning, get my nails and feet done, as usual. Then me and Trenice might go shopping and out to lunch. Why?"

"We havin' a barbecue at one of Chill's houses. I wanted to see if you wanted to go."

"Who is *we*?" I was curious.

"Me, Chill, M1, and da fellas, a few of our…. Just a bunch of people."

Oh, yeah, girls in bikinis and shit. I was most definitely going to be there. I know all about that beach shit. I've been fucked in the pool before!

"Yeah, I'll go. But I ain't gonna be there all day and night."

Yeah right! Long as your ass is there, I'll be there too.

"Well it starts around two and end whenever. You can ride with me, or you can drive your own whip and meet me there. 'Cause I'll be there early settin' up da grill and shit."

"Well, I'll meet you there then."

He smirked. "Yeah, dat's straight." He got naked, "I'm finna take a shower so I can lay down. I'm tired as fuck." I watched him go in the bathroom.

If something is going on, I'll find out tomorrow. I want to be as close as possible to his environment so I can see what's going on in his world. I want to find out why he ain't been begging for this pussy.

CHAPTER 20

FRIDAY NIGHT
ROUSEAU

I've been spending any time I have trying to pump my gamblin' house back up, to get niggas to trust me once again. It's been hard to get niggas to feel comfortable once again. But I've done everything possible, especially beefing up my security team. I've added walkie talkies and people on the roof. I've lost a lot of income due to my slippage. But one thing for sure is that I know how to bounce back. I've been sitting in this office going over my figures for the month.

<Knock knock>

"Yeah!" I called out. "Come in!"

"Bossman, I don't mean to interrupt you, but it's some cat out here wants to talk to you."

"What nigga? Who is he?"

"I don't know, but we patted him down. He straight. He say he has some important info for you." He waited for my response.

"Important info? Yeah, right. Send the nigga in and stand by."

Some young, wild-looking nigga walked in the office. I've never seen this cat before in my life. He sat down, and we watched each other. I sized jit up. He was about 5'9", medium built, with wickeds (dreads) that came to the middle of his shoulder blades and were turning red on the tips. His eyes were red an' glossy.

"What's you name, dawg?"

"They call me Taterhead." His mouth was full of gold teeth.

"How you know me?"

"I don't know you personally, but I know *of* you," he responded.

I didn't say anything, just watched him for a second.

"So what type of info you got, and why you think I want to hear it?"

"Because it's about you and a robbery dat happened to you."

I grinded my jaws together. The inside of my stomach was turning, but I showed no visible reaction.

"So you have information about a robbery that supposedly happened to me?"

"No, not supposedly. I know it happened."

"Oh, yeah, and how you know that?" I sat back and waited.

"I know 'cause I was one of da ones who robbed you."

Buddha pulled out his fire in a flash and aimed it at the young nigga's head. The nigga ain't flinch and kept his eyes on me.

"My nigga, I just came back from da dead, and I don't mind dyin' again. But you won't never get what you want if I don't give it to you."

I nodded my head – smart young nigga. Another time, another place, I coulda used jit on my team.

I signaled Buddha to lower his gat.

"So you woke up today and decided to come clean. What? You suddenly had a change of heart, nigga?"

"My nigga," he shrugged, "my reasons for robbin' you, I don't know you, it was strictly business. Dey came wit' da come-up, and I was down for it. I know you been on da right side of da fire befo', my nigga. So you know what it's like. But my reasons for comin' ta holla at you, well, it's not business; it's personal."

I looked over at Buddha, who look like he wanted to erase jit off the map. I sat back and thought about the situation. I can't knock a nigga for the come-up. Shit, I was once that nigga, and besides, I wanted to get to the bottom of this shit and this cat may be the key. If need be, I could take care of him later.

"And what you want in return for your info? I know you ain't telling me you gonna give me something for nothin'. Ain't nothin' in life free, young buck. So unless you're tryin' to get right with God and cleanse your soul, why don't you tell me what's the quid pro quo."

I'm smart enough to know that something is going on behind the scenes. Meaning he fell out with his homeboys. It sound like they beefin'. I would like to know for sure, but in the scheme of things, what's important is that I get what I need.

"What's to stop me from gettin' the info from you then doing something to you before you leave?" I questioned.

"Because somebody followed me here, and now they parked somewhere waiting. And if I don't hit 'em up in thirty minutes, den dey know to get da crackas involved," he explained.

"And how do I know you're not lying, using me to handle some beef you got with some niggas I don't even know?"

"Because when I tell you da names, you a know I ain't shooting you nuttin' fugazi, you boy!" His first true show of emotion.

"Alright, let's have it then," I was ready.

"You ain't even tell me if we had a deal or not."

"Homeboy, you made it this far. So you can assume we have a deal. I'm a man of my word. Let's hope that you're a man of yours. So, now, what's the names?" I was getting impatient.

"It's two names: Chill and M1." He looked me in the eye.

Muthafuckas!

"M1 is Ch –"

I cut him off, "I know who the fuck M1 is!"

"Dose are da niggas dat touched you."

"So you telling me that Chill is back in the robbin' game? I know the nigga ain't fell off. Shit, from what I'm hearing, the l'il nigga gettin' money in a major way. If it's him, it's got to be more to the story. I need to know everything you know from start to finish, and then you can go. But I need every name and detail – everything."

Muthafucka!

"It ain't no *if*. It's them. I'll tell you how it went down. Chill come..."

———

I've been sitting in my office all night going over everything that young nigga told me, plus everything I already know. I still can't believe this shit. I'm trying to find the motive, but all I can think of, besides natural dislike, is maybe they found out about me steppin' on their toes with Trap and that paperwork. But it that enough? I let a lot of shit slide in my day. Some battles just ain't worth it. But the l'il nigga Taterhead had it right earlier when he said this is personal.

My own l'il cousin… I know if Chill is involved he has to be involved. It's a shame, but I'm gonna teach these niggas a lesson. I got to, or I'll feel less than a man. The question was just how. This has to be done just right 'cause they gonna remember this. They want war, I'm gonna give it to 'em. But it's not like any war they've ever been in. It's gonna be a mental war!

CHAPTER 21

SATURDAY, 4TH OF JULY
CHILL/JAP/SHAY

CHILL

"Damn Jap, what's takin' so long wit' dat grub, nigga?" M1 hollered at Jap.

"Hold up, ol' hungry-ass nigga!" Jap called back.

We were at the house that we had rented for the girls. We were thinking about the beach, but this was the perfect locale. I definitely wasn't going to let 'em know where the Big House was. But over here, the backyard was huge and included a pool, Jacuzzi, screened-in patio, three island huts, volleyball area with beach sand, and plenty of land. I had leased something that would keep the girls very comfortable for the six months we planned on running this operation.

Everybody was there – the girls, M1, the fellas, Lauren, and Shay. It was a beautiful day. We had the grill goin' and people in the water, playing volleyball. We were all smokin' purp and drinkin' plenty of liq.

"Fuck dat, pass dat joint and stop babysittin'," I told M1.

"Nigga, roll yo' own. I brought half a pound of haze for dat purpose. Nigga, I ain't sharin'," he responded.

Some of the girls was playing volleyball, Lauren and Shay were talking, and us niggas were drinking, smokin', and talkin' shit. Except for Chaunce and Goon who, I couldn't believe, let the girls talk them into playing volleyball. We had the music bumpin' out the outdoor speakers, which were disguised as fake rocks.

Everyone was decked out in nice summer wear. All the women had on expensive, designer bikinis. A couple had on see-through wraps. The fellas were laid back. M1 had on a Polo short set. Chaunce and Goon had on a Nike shorts with wife beaters. Jap had on jean shorts, no shirt, and flip flops, and I had on a Nautica yachting short set.

"Damn, well somebody roll one up for the da cook," Jap insisted.

"Nah, nah… Cook can't hit da weed 'til he finished dat food on da grill!" everyone shouted.

I poured a couple of martinis and walked off toward Lauren and Shay.

"What's up, ladies? I'm at your service. I've come to refresh your drinks," I said, in my best English accent. They giggled.

"Thank you, Mante', Lauren told me, and hugged me with one arm.

"Yeah, thanks, Chill," Shay added. "Jap still over there playing on that grill?"

"Yeah, but he got some meat coming off soon...I hope!"

"Let me go see if he needs some help. I'll be back, Lauren." She left us alone.

"What dey do, Miss Lady? Are you enjoyin' yourself?" I asked her, as we took a seat under the hut where Shay and she were standing.

"Yeah, I'm having a really good time. I'm glad, *very* glad, Arthur had a business trip and that I could make it."

"Dat makes two of us. It's still early." I glanced at my Nautica marine watch. "Three o'clock, it's going to get a lot more exciting."

———

"Hey y'all, come and get it. Dis food hot and ready to go," Jap finally called out.

"'Bout time, nigga! Niggas' stomachs touchin' dey backs," Chaunce admitted.

Everybody came from playing volleyball, jumped out the pool and Jacuzzi, and made a run for the hut where the dining tables and benches were located. I had whipped up the potato salad and baked beans 'cause I'm not only a mack, I'm a chef. Lauren made the mac and cheese from scratch. It was a grubfest with plenty of drink.

Everybody talkin', laughin', and havin' a good time. That's when a glimpse of things to come started to present itself. While everyone was at the table eating, Jap went back to the grill to check on the rest of the meat. Destiny walked over to Jap, kissed him on the cheek, told him he did his thang on the grill, smacked him on the ass, and walked off.

Lauren tapped my leg under the table.

"What's up, sweetie?" I looked at Lauren seated next to me, looking at me as if Jap had just committed the number one sin.

"Did you see that?" she asked.

"See what?"

"That girl just kissed Jap on the cheek and patted his ass." I looked up at Jap, then we both looked over at Shay, and she looked fire hot.

"Shit, did it look outta line?"

"I don't know, it looked like something."

———

SHAY

I walked up to Jap. I said between clenched teeth, "What the fuck was that, Jap?"

He had the nerve to look at me confused.

"What?"

"You know what the fuck I'm talking about. That bitch that just palmed your ass."

"Man, she was just saying good job on the food. You know, in sports you pat your teammate on da ass, girl." He explained with his hands out like, "What's the big deal?".

"Nigga, this ain't sports, and she sure as hell ain't your teammate. Matter of fact, I think I'll let her know myself!" I made to go confront that bitch.

He grabbed my wrist and pulled me back.

"Don't fuck da party up ova bullshit. Everybody having a good time. I'll handle it."

I looked at him.

"You make sure you do!" I stalked off and poured myself a drink.

———

After everybody ate, me and Chill put da rest of da meat and food on da grill to stay warm, in case people got hungry again as the night went on. Shay and Lauren assisted us, while Goon and Chaunce had a spade game going on wit' L'il bit and Talia. Some of the others was playin' drunken basketball in the pool. The rest were just loungin' 'round grinnin', sippin' and relaxin'.

"Oh, yeah, nigga. I heard shit earlier. When l'il momma grabbed dat ass," he mentioned, when da girls headed to the kitchen to put shit up.

"I dont' know what dat was about. I ain't think nothin' of it, everybody drinkin' and shit. She probably just feelin' good or somethin'!"

"I don't know, boy. You never know," he looked at me, then at da meat. "Man, dat shit straight for now. I'm finna go jump off in da pool on dis water-ball. What dey do?"

"Yeah, I'm wit' dat."

We headed over to the pool.

———

SHAY

That shit with Jap and that bitch was still on my mind as me and Lauren put the potato salad in the fridge and got more ice for the coolers.

"Damn it," I dropped all the damn ice on the floor.

"You alright, girl?" Lauren asked.

"Yeah, girl. Did you – I know you saw that disrespectful-ass shit that bitch pulled with Jap."

"I saw it, but don't make too much out of it. She probably is just feeling her alcohol and didn't realize what she was doing."

"Don't make too much out of it?. How can you say that? You don't even have a husband!"

She looked at me hard.

"I'm sorry, Lauren. Look, to be honest, the last month has been very stressful on my marriage."

I really like Lauren. She made it so easy to talk to her.

"I'm so embarrassed to be telling you this, but Jap and I haven't had sex in about a month."

She raised her eyebrows.

"I don't want to pry. Do you want to talk about it?" She inquired out of concern.

I told her what happened.

"Not trying to belittle your feelings, but maybe he is telling the truth," she stated, once I finished.

"I thought about that. It's just that we've been married for over three years, and this has never happened. And... I don't know, maybe it's just my pride that's hurt. I mean I know what his job entails, and I can't say I don't reap the benefits. I just... I don't know. Just like with the shit that happened today, it might not have been his fault, but it still makes me resentful towards him," I confided, as we picked up the last of the ice.

"Listen, deep in your heart, you know Jap. You know he wouldn't do anything to disrespect or jeopardize your marriage. Don't let your foolish pride cloud your judgment. You have a very good husband and now is the time to give him the benefit of the doubt."

She actually brought tears to my eyes. She reached out and hugged me.

"Thank you, Lauren. I don't know what I was doing, but you're absolutely right. Tonight, when I get home, I'm going to show him how much I love him," I shook my head. "When is Chill going to realize you're all he needs?"

"He will, soon enough."

We grabbed fresh ice and picked up the sodas and began to head back outside.

My cell phone started ringing.

"I'll be right there, Lauren. This is my best friend Trenice."

It was FB – couldn't tell her that.

"Ok, you're fine now?"

"Yes, I'm okay. Thanks to you," I let her know.

She walked out. I answered.

———

CHILL

We were out in the pool playing basketball. Me, Poca, Heaven, and Spice were against Jap, Destiny, Selena, and Mya. We were in fun-filled grudge match, while M1, Cheyenne, and Passion cheered us on sittin' under a hut, sippin' and smokin'. We were fourteen to thirteen in a game going to fifteen when I hit a long-range shot that gave our team the victory.

"Good shot, Chill!" Heaven high-fived me.

"Hell, yeah! We beat they ass!" added Spice with another high-five.

"Yeah, boo! Good game," Poca told me, then kissed me in the mouth – all tongue.

Whoooa!

She let me go, winked, and swam to the other side of the pool. My dick got hard off that one l'il kiss. It got to be the atmosphere 'cause she ain't ever vibe with me like that. Fuck it, everybody havin' a good time.

"I see ya, boy," Jap teased as he swam up.

"You know it's da liq. Bitches just vibin' and shit."

"I 'on know, boy. Dat shit had a l'il somethin' behind it."

"Nah, ain't nuttin' serious, fool. She woulda been got at me years ago."

"You wasn't what you are now years ago."

Made sense!

———

"Damn, I'm gonna pee on myself," Lauren whispered to herself as she speed-walked back inside the house to the bathroom. When she got there, the door was closed. She raised her hands to knock, when she heard a voice talking low. She turned to leave and go to the other bathroom, but she heard the voice moan, and she realized she recognized the voice. She grew concerned and started to yell through the door to ask if everything was ok, until she heard, "Stop it, you make me wet when you talk like that," Shay whispered loudly in the manner that tipsy people do. I told you, I'm the bathroom, boy, sitting on the toilet lid."

"Oh, yeah. Then what?" She heard asked.

"Um, shit. That sounds good."

"I wanna stroke it myself right now," she responded to whatever he said.

"'Cause I can't. Somebody might hear me. You know how loud I am."

"I'll do my best. Fuck it… Put that tongue on ice. I promise I'll see you later.

"Oooh, baby, yeah… I'm gonna pee on you. My pussy throbbin' just thinkin' about it."

"Yes, I promise. I'm gonna call you when I can get free. Tell my l'il friend I'll talk to him later."

Lauren moved her face from the door and quickly went back outside. She forgot she had to use the bathroom. "What should I do?" she thought. She had to talk to someone. She couldn't possibly tell Jap. She had to find Chill.

CHILL

We were all sitting round burnin' purp and tellin' jokes. M1 was telling us a story about this one-legged female named Trenae that he had sex with.

"I ain't gonna lie. She had some good-ass pussy. When she nutted, her l'il stub went to shakin' like a muhfucka!" He demonstrated.

Everyone bust out laughin'.

"Cous', you a nasty-ass nigga," Poca teased through her laughter.

"No, I ain't. I'm a trendsetter. You two-legged bitches played out!"

Hey, my dawg stupid as fuck! He had us all rolling.

I was smokin' with Poca sittin' on my lap. We were sittin' in a big circle under one of the huts. I had my back facing the house. Poca was sittin' sideways on my lap, so she could see behind me to the house.

"Damn, Chill, you ain't gonna let me hit ya joint?" We had five J's burnin' in Backwoods and. TI "24's" playin' on the speakers.

"Yeah, you could hit it, stop trippin'," I told her before I hit it again.

She grabbed it from my lips, "Chill, let me give you a shotgun."

Before I could respond, she hit the weed, held the smoke, put her mouth against mine, blew smoke in my mouth, and hit me with a l'il tongue play.

"Dat's a hell of a shotgun, Poca!" exclaimed an excited Mya.

"Let da nigga breathe, bitch!" added L'il Bit.

"I know, right!" chimed in a smiling Spice.

"Damn, cous'," M1 said loudly, "You 'posed to be givin' my nigga a shotty, not try and suck his fuckin' tonsils out!"

"Chill?"

I broke the kiss off, puffed my cheeks out, and turned sideways so Lauren could see whatever smoke I had left.

"What's up, sweetie?" I answered in a smoke-filled voice.

"I need to talk to you for a minute."

I could see her concealing her emotions. I turned back 'round to a smiling Pocahontas.

Slick-ass bitch. Think she got all the sense.

"Let me get up, l'il momma," I requested smoothly, also concealing my feelings about her playin' on a real nigga intelligence.

She stood up slowly, and I got up to head off with Lauren.

"Lauren, where Shay at?"

"Oh, she – she's using the bathroom," she stuttered. "She should be out in a minute." She looked at me.

She turned and walked off in front of me.

That was strange. She sounded uncomfortable. I thought it was because of me and Poca a minute ago. But a few minutes later I'd find out.

"I tried to beat her to the punch," Sweetie, Poca was just giv – "She cut me off.

"Mante', I know I'm not your girl. You don't owe me any explanation."

"I just wanted to let you know it ain't even like that. I wouldn't invite you somewhere and shit on you. You feel me? Girlfriend or not, I wouldn't try you like that. I'm betta than dat."

She watched me, then took a deep breath, "I know, Mante'. I also know that Pocahontas has a serious thing for you. She's been watching you all day. I can feel the lust she has for you. It's intense."

"Hell, nah! She just drunk and high and feelin' good, that's all. Ain't no big deal.

"Mante'," I've never known you to be one for being naive, so don't start now," she scolded. "Anyway, that's not why I brought you here." A look of concern passed her face.

I moved closer and put my arms around her shoulders.

"What's up, l'il momma. What's on ya mind?"

"I heard something a few minutes ago that I wasn't supposed to, and I don't know what to do about it, so I'm bringing it to you."

"You know I'm always here for you. So tell me what it is you heard."

"I heard Shay having phone sex in the bathroom," she paused.

I frowned, "Say what?" I said, while rubbin' my Goatee with a confused expression on my face.

"At first I thought it was a mistake. I mean I wanted to be mistaken, but I'm not. She looked away from me and shook her head.

My heart was beating fast. I was shocked.

"What you… What exactly did you hear? I'm not questionin' your story, but this is some crazy shit. I just wanna be sure," I explained.

She told me everything.

My suspicions were confirmed. But this shit here, this was some ol' other type shit. Yeah, I'm a pee on you! What type of shit is dat?

"Mante', you have to tell him! I can't break Jap's heart like that."

"Shit, what make you think I wanna break it?" I shot back.

"Baby, you know that's not what I meant. I just… I know it would be better coming from his best friend."

"Man, I 'on know 'bout dat, Lauren. Dat shit don't sound right comin' from anybody. And I ain't want to get in the middle of that," I reasoned.

"I'm not understanding."

"Dat shit could go either way. I might tell a nigga dat shit, and he might start resenting me, or he might not even believe it. He got his head stuck in his ass when it comes to Shay."

"Yeah… You're right, Mante'."

"I mean if they stay together, I've created an enemy in Shay. Even though I don't give a fuck. But me and Jap vibe gonna be fucked up. And shit would most definitely hinder our business."

"So what do we do? Just don't say anything? Let her get away with something like this?"

"Just let me sleep on it for a couple days and I'll decide somethin'," I scratched my head. You straight?"

"Yeah, I'm cool. It's just that I hate to see something like this happen to a friend, or anyone for that matter."

I smiled and pinched her chin, "Always thinkin' 'bout others, huh? I like that."

"Oh, but you wouldn't like it if we were married and you tried some shit like that," she stated firmly.

"Why you say dat?"

"'Cause I'd cut your dick off and stuff it in your mouth. After that, I'd leave you."

Ouch!

"I always knew you had another side to you, just

208

waitin' ta break free," I joked, "But you don't have to worry about dat anyway, sweetie."

"Why? 'Cause you love me so much?"

"Nah, 'Cause you got tabs on my damn money. I gotta keep you happy!"

She hit me in the chest and snuggled in close.

"Baby, you're so silly," she giggled and hugged me tight.

In the distance, Pocahontas watched in envy.

———

CHAPTER 22

It was now 11:00 at night. The sun was gone, and everyone was a lot less inhibited. Poca and her gang had popped tic-tacs (ecstasy pills) and were now topless. They were windin' and grindin', strip teasin' and playin' with each other to the R. Kelly "TP2.com" album. We brought out bottles of Cristal. The fellas sat back and enjoyed the show.

"Mante', it's late, and I have a long drive to Coconut Grove. I should get started, before I get sleepy. I'm already tired and half drunk," Lauren acknowledged.

I knew that wasn't the only reason she was leaving. I knew she was also uncomfortable with the direction the party was headed. But she wouldn't be a party pooper and mention that. That wasn't her style. She was more subtle than that.

I got an idea.

"Lauren, why don't you just stay at The Big House tonight? It's a lot closer, and I'll feel safer than having you drive way to da Grove."

"So what? I can be there all by myself?" she tested.

I caught the underlying meaning in her words. So did everyone else.

"You won't be by yourself. I wouldn't do you like that. I'll be there in a couple of hours.

She looked deep into my eyes. Both of us knew what the other was implying. And we knew what each other wanted. With alcohol surging through our systems, the feelings we already shared were amplified.

She stood up, stepped in front of me, and looked down. "Are you gonna walk me to the car?"

She said goodnight to Shay and the fellas and we headed to her vehicle. Before she got in the car, she kissed me and said, "Mante', I want you next to me tonight. Please, don't keep me waiting forever."

I looked her in the eye. "I won't, baby, I won't."

When I got back, M1 confronted me. "Oh, Mante, I don't want to be all alone!" he mimicked Lauren. "Fool, you betta tighten up. I woulda left wit' her. Fuck dat. But den again, it's some bad bitches here. Shit, I'll fuck somethin' here to get dat first nut off, my nigga. Dat way when I get to da crib wit' Lauren, I won't nut too fast, you feel me? A nigga gotta make a good impression da first time. Can't do da quickie thang, my nigga. All ya pussy a be ranked."

I gave my nigga dap. He don't sugacoat nuttin'. Da nigga a fool!

———

L'SHAY

My goodness! I followed the conversation between Lauren and Chill. They act like they wanted to fuck right here and now. I could feel the sexual tension in the air. But since Lauren made her exit, I'm gonna use that as an excuse to make mine. My mind keeps going back to the conversation me and FB had. I know my bikini is stained with juices up under this wrap. But the talk me and Lauren had did make me feel kind of guilty for the way I've been treating Jap. Don't get me wrong, my husband isn't bad in bed, but he don't do the things FB do. And right now, with the way I'm feeling, I'm on that freaky, piss-on-a-nigga, stick-a-finger-in-my-ass type shit. Jap and I ain't had sex in a month, and I don't feel like going through all the tension. So a bitch like me need to make a run for the border.

"Jap, baby... I'm gonna go ahead and leave, too. I have to stop at Walgreen's and pick up medicine for Trenice. She got real sick while we were out earlier. I talked to her a while ago and told her I'd go to the twenty-four-hour Walgreen's before I stopped by her house," I gamed him.

"You need me to go wit' you?"

"No, baby. I'm not gonna fuck up your fun, for once. Besides, you know I'm going to sit with her a while and have girl talk."

"I forgot about that. Well, shit, I ain't gonna be too far behind you."

I got up, crossed to him, and sat on his lap. I kissed him good, but not so much that it would make him want to come with me.

"Call me when you're on your way home and I'll meet you there, baby."

I got up and grabbed his hand so he'd follow me to the car. Once there, I kissed him bye, got in my car, and hauled ass! Soon as I got down the street, I called FB, 'cause I was ready – so ready. I hope Jap gives me at least a couple hours. I need time to fuck all this shit out my system.

———

CHILL

I sat there and listened to the bullshit Shay just ran on my homeboy. That shit got me hot, my nigga. Normally, I would've paid little or no attention, but since Lauren put me up on game, my antennae were vibratin' left and right.

M1 got up and sat next to me.

"I see you peeped dat play, too. All dat shit was fugazi," he whispered.

"Yeah, I know. Lauren told me some shit earlier, too."

I ran it down.

"So you gonna holla at buddy, or what?" he inquired.

"My nigga, I on' know fool. I'm a let it marinate for a couple of days before I decide."

"Yeah, I feel you, fool. A nigga don't wanna get in all dat marriage business and shit, but buddy need to know." He looked at me. "Shit, I'll run it down if you want," he smiled.

"Hell, nah… You too harsh, my nigga. A nigga need a l'il finesse on dis shit cause his feelings gonna be hurt and shit."

"I dig it. In da meantime, grab one of dem bottles of Cris, nigga. Let's go out here and get loose wit' da hoes."

We went over by the pool where the girls were dancing, in and out. Chaunce and Goon followed.

"I see cous' been vibin' on you all day. What dat be 'bout?"

"Lauren said da same shit. I just charged it to da liquor."

He smirked and shook his head.

"Nah, I know my fam. I think it's more dan dat, but we'll rap later."

Soon as we got over there, they started dancing on and around us.

"'Bout time y'all came this way. We thought y'all was scared of pussy or somethin'," L'il Bit cracked.

"Pussy won't kill me! Only make me stronger!" I yelled back at her.

Me and M1 dapped up, grabbed a few ass cheeks, filled our glasses and joked a little bit.

I'm glad his little friend or whoever she is finally decided to leave. Now I can show him a good time, and express my feelings, without having to compete for his attention. I danced seductively as I eased towards him, hands raised over my head. I kept his eye contact, put my arms around his neck, and pushed my naked breasts against his chest as I grinded my pelvis into him.

I'd watched him grow up from elementary. He went from the boy with the big head and big lips to one of the sexiest niggas I know. I've been in relationship after relationship and not one had completely satisfied me. I deserved better! I deserved the best. I'm tired of breaking my neck for niggas and getting shitted on. Yeah, I know I've stripped before and, hell, even did some tricking. But I used what was available to me and did what I had to, in order to make a way for myself. I'm nothing if not wifey material.

I took whatever money I hustled up, paid my way through college and got a degree. I paid for my acting classes, and, although I'm not a big-time actress, I've been in commercials, videos, and had a couple small roles in movies. At twenty-five, I have a lot to offer. I have my own house, car, and I'm ambitious. I just need someone to compliment my qualities. I wish I had someone like Chill. Better yet, I wish I had Chill. You know what, why shouldn't I have him? I deserve it, and he deserves me. He's a king, and it's about time he had a queen – a real queen – not that bourgeois bitch that was here earlier. Don't get me wrong. She's a sexy female. *I* wouldn't mind fucking her. But I can tell she's from a different world than him. He needs someone who can understand him, understand the mind of the hustlin'-ass nigga that he is!

He needs me.

I'll be damned if he doesn't know it tonight.

I felt Mya grinding on my ass. As she brought me out of my reverie, I turned around, grinded my ass on Chill, and let Mya suck my nipples. I caught the eyes of all my girls, who were like me, high, drunk, rolling, and horny. They were all grindin' on dick or each other. They knew what time it was. I pulled down Mya's bikini bottom. All the rest followed suit.

"Dat's what da fuck I'm talkin' 'bout!" M1 joked wit' the bottle of Cris and a joint to chase it. "Real niggas ain't even gotta ask! Da panties just fall off by dey muhfuckin' self!"

Poca reached behind her and started strokin' my dick. She used her other hand to guide my hand all over her ass and between her split, while her and Mya kissed.

Then Heaven yelled out, "Last one in the pool don't get no pussy!"

Girl started diving in the pool. Da fellas dove in clothes, shoes, and all, just as Jap came back and asked, "Wha da fuck y'all got goin' on?" He had a big Kool-aid smile on his face.

M1 yelled at him, "You don't get no pussy, Jap!"

"Uh-uh, shawty! You get all the punany you want!" Destiny assured.

She climbed out the pool. Destiny was beautiful in her birthday suit. She was pork 'n' beans brown, pigeon toed, with an ass round like two 24-inch tires. She had titties like two coconuts, and a pussy that hang like four niggas on a corner. She had a face like Keyshia Cole, and she wanted Jap.

"Let me handle that for you," she kneeled in front of him.

He just stared at her. It looked like he wanted to stop her or say somethin', but all eyes were on him. No time to flaw out. She stripped him down to his boxers, at the same time, the rest of us had girls undressing us. She led him into the pool. We had that Trick Daddy "Book of Thugs" album playin' on the outdoor system.

Yeah, talk dat gangsta, freaky shit, fool.

They was puttin' on a mean show for us. M1 was sandwiched between Selena and Mya, Passion cornered off Chaunce, and Poca roped me off.

I heard L'il Bit tell Goon, "Yeah, nigga, I'm a see if you circumcised tonight."

Talia jumped out the water and said she'd be right back.

She came back with a Dooney 'n Bourke duffel. All the girls squealed. Cheyenne, Heaven, and Spice climbed out the pool. Talia laid a big beach towel on the grass, at the side of the pool.

"We got a surprise for y'all," Cheyenne told us, while lookin' down at us in the pool.

"Um-hum," acknowledged Heaven.

"Hurry up. I'm horny," Spice rubbed on Talia.

"Watch this, baby." Poca leaned back against me and whispered while she kept hold of my dick.

Talia emptied the contents of the bag. Every nigga eyebrows was touchin' their hairline. The bag had an assortment of dildos, strap-ons, bottles of motion lotion, big and small beads, ticklers, whips, and other sex toys even *I* didn't recognize.

Let the party begin.

———

CHAPTER 23

Lauren had just made it to Chill's house. She got her overnight bag out the trunk. Mante' didn't know it, but she had planned this all along. If he wouldn't have offered, then she would've suggested it. It was time, and she was more than ready. She climbed the stairs to his bedroom suite. Once there, she took the special lingerie that she bought, just for him, out of the bag. "I love him! This night is going to be special. We need this. This is our future," she thought, as she entered the bathroom to shower.

———

JAP

"Damn girl, dat feel good," I whispered softly as she stroked my dick underwater, at the same time suckin' on my earlobe and kissin' my neck. I switched between closin' my eyes and watchin' da freak show on da grass. I ain't been touched in so long, I was finna skeet, just on her hand play.

"You like dat, shawty?" She asked in my ear.

Poca and Destiny had gotten together with their plans earlier and were dead set on makin' it happen.

So far, so good.

"Come on," she grabbed my hand. "I want to show you somethin'."

We climbed out da pool. I was followin' my dick. She stopped at da hut and grabbed a bottle of Cris and some weed. I followed da ass.

———

CHILL

I was shocked as fuck. I saw my nigga goin' to fuck somethin'. Hell nah! I know I gotta be fucked up. But dat nigga deserve it. He ain't fuck nothin' new since before he got married. My dawg gave up his hoeish ways, and she got the nerve to be fuckin', suckin', and givin' niggas golden showers.

Pussy-ass hoe! Get yours, fool. I thought as…

Oh! Shit!

So wet, so hot.

I ain't talkin' water.

Poca had slipped me in the pussy while I zoned out. I reached 'round and grabbed her titties.

"O…o…oh, Chill," she reached back and grabbed my hips, "I been waiting for this, forever."

"Yeeaah?" I started slow strokin'.

She stepped forward and turned around.

"Man, why you playin', girl?" I asked impatiently. "Come here."

"This is our first time," she stepped back in the zone and grabbed my monster. "I want to be alone wit' that." She looked down, then back in my face.

"Well, shit… Let's go," I insisted.

She stuck her tongue in my mouth, let me go, climbed out, and waited for me to follow. She grabbed my hand and led the way. I looked at the scene I was leaving. Three niggas and eight females. They're gonna be loose out here. Oh, well… Been there, done that, and will be back once again. I'm a handle Poca. Then I gotta get home to Lauren. I can't stand her up.

I won't stand her up.

———

SHAY

"Ooooh, aahhhh, fu...c...k my p...uss...y... nu..." I half-yelled, half-shivered.

"Don't stop, don't stop!" Every nerve in my body was sending out sparks. "Slap my ass!" Whack. "Ouch, ow, again!" Whack. "Uhhh, fuck!"

"Yeah, bitch, back dat pussy up!" FB commanded, while he pulled my hair, making me arch my back. "Take dat dick, bitch! Grip it with dat pussy. Uh, hm... Just like dat, yeah!"

"Uhh, uhh... Hurt that pussy... Hurt your fat freaky pussy!" I cried out.

"Yeah, yeah! Make Poppa nut! Make me nut, girl!"

I used my coochie muscles and gripped his dick tightly while he fucked me from behind. I felt like a wild bitch in the street the way he was mounting me. I felt so nasty.

I felt so good!

"Poppa, I'm cumming again!" I hollered.

"Louder, bitch! I can't hear you."

"Ohhhh, Poppa! I'm cumming on your fat dick."

"Yeeaah, bitch! I'm cumming with you."

"Cum with me! Umm... Cum with me!"

We both screamed, grunted, and gasped out in excitement as we climaxed together. Round 1 was in the books. Now it was time for two, three, or ten.

————

JAP

"You like that, baby?" She asked. I lay on my back while she sucked on my nipples.

"Yeah, dat shit feel good." She proceeded to kiss down my stomach and lick the shaft of my dick. When her mouth wrapped around the head of my dick, and she popped it out, with a l'il poppin' sound behind it, my toes curled. I watched her and she watched me right back, eye to eye. But when she spit on the tip of my l'il sword, and took him all the way to the back of her throat, no gag reflex, I nearly lost my damn mind.

"Oh, shit, girl," I panted, "You gonna make...uh...I'm a nut right in yo' mouth!"

She paused right at the tip, and I could feel her warm breath as she said, "Well, what you waitin' on, shawty?" She sucked even faster.

My back arched as I grabbed her head and started fuckin' her face. My eyes closed as I inched closer and closer to skeetin'. I opened my eyes so I could see her swallow every drop. But it wasn't her face I saw. It was Shay's.

I lost all momentum.

"Stop," I told her, halfway to panickin'. I tried to lift her face off of me.

"Get up. I can't do dis! Dis shit ain't right."

But she maintained her rhythm and squeezed me between her tongue and the roof of her mouth, while her lips covered her teeth.

"No, no, Dest -- ahh," I cried out. The harder I lifted, the harder she pressed down. I tried to shove my dick in her mouth hard and pull her hair harder, to get her off me. Little did I know, dat aggressive shit was right up her alley.

She used two fingers to massage a spot behind my nuts dat I didn't even know about.

"Ohhh, shit, ummm!" I hollered like a bitch, "Nooo, I can... ummm!"

I came like I never came before. Every muscle in my body locked up. She drank it all. When she finished, she said, "I knew you could do it." She licked her lips, "You drank a lot of orange juice, huh?" She giggled playfully and crawled up next to me. I felt damn good, but I felt so bad. How could I have done dis to Shay?. I broke the promises of my marriage.

———

SHAY

"Spank me harder, you pussy! Slap me with the belt!" I was on my hands and knees in the middle of the bed, while FB stood over me whipping because I was dirty and nasty. Ooh, so dirty and nasty!

"Yeah, bitch! Reach up under there and stroke dat clit while I spank you, you dirty bitch!" Whack.

"Ummm, yeah, Poppa! I'm dirty, Poppa!" Whack. "Oh fuck! Fuck you, Poppa!" Whack. "Uhhh, urgghh!" He grabbed a handful of my hair, and pulled back so I had an automatic arch in my back.

Whack!

"Yeah, dat fat ass turnin' red, you feel dat?" Whack. "Ooo, ohh, Poppa! I'm cuuumminnngg!" With that last slap, my pussy unleashed everything it held. I squirted my juices all over the bed. I looked down between my legs to watch. I loved to watch myself cum. It made me feel so sexy.

"Come on, Poppa! Fuck me while I'm cumming," I pleaded, "Put it in, ummm, put it in!"

He did just that. He grabbed two hands full of hair and rode out on my ass. He was jamming me so hard his nuts slapped up against my clit.

Do it Poppa! Do it!

———

CHILL

"Baby, just lay down and let me take care of you," Poca said, softly and pleasingly. She lit candles around the bedroom.

"I've been waiting so long for this, Chill. I know you're probably surprised about my feelings for you." She eased on the bed with a bottle of motion lotion. "I didn't know how to tell you, and I didn't know what you'd think or feel, so I kept my feelings to myself." She straddled my back.

I was lying face-down in massage position. I heard her uncap the bottle. The thick, cool liquid, that smelled of strawberries, hit my back.

"I want you, Chill," she whispered in my ear, while she rubbed the lotion in all over my back. "I want you all for myself." She began grindin' her plump, bald pussy into the small of my back, kissing and blowing different spots on my back. Everywhere her breath hit, the lotion heated up. Soon, I was biting my bottom lip and moaning like a muhfucka. Her pussy had the bottom of my back wetter than the lotion.

She slid down and placed her body between my legs. Then she poured more of the lotion on my legs. She massaged both legs at the same time, emphasizing the inner thighs.

"I'm in love with you, Chill." I heard her, but I was feeling too good to pay attention to that.

"Oh, yeah? Show me," I replied knowing that those tic-tacs was probably giving her that lovey, dovey feeling.

She poured lotion on my ass cheeks and began to massage. I know she ain't finna try me wit' dat finger- in-the-ass game. I opened my eyes and came up out of my bliss.

"Poca, I aint' wit' dat fuck shit. We go way back, but I'll still slide you ass 'bout tryin' me!"

She giggled and slapped my ass.

"Boy, I know better than that."

She began to add kisses to the massage. Had a nigga cheeks hot.

"Chill?" She called, in a low voice.

"Yeah, girl?" I answered back.

"Chill?"

"What's my name, baby?"

"Hm?" I answered, confused.

"Tell me my name."

"Pocahontas. Why?"

She took her tongue and licked da whole length of my ass crack. I instantly locked up, but she still went to work with her tongue.

She paused just to ask me one more question before she continued, "What's my name, Chill?"

"Po..ca..hon..tas," I managed to gasp out of the breath I'd been holding while her tongue licked circles around my asshole.

Dookie love!

———

SHAY

I was laying on my back with my feet cocked all the way back, like I was going to do a backflip. He was in push-up position, on top of me, facing the opposite direction and giving me a gold medal pounding. I stroked his nuts and pushed down on his ass while he beat away. We were both sweaty and drained, but still going. See, this is the shit Jap can't do.

I've never been in this position!

<Ring ring ring>

Damn! Damn! Damn! That has to be Jap.

No! No! No! Not now!

"You...wanna...get...dat?" he asked, while he continued to hit it.

"I'm...kind...of...tied...up...uuhhh...uhhh... uhhh," I squealed out.

Fuck! Why does he have to call now? Not now!

"Ahhh!" I yelled out in pain and pleasure as FB shoved two fingers in my ass while he balanced on one hand.

Amazing!

"Your ass is wet, just like your pussy."

<Ring Ring Ring>

"Keep going, don't stop! Keep going, Poppa! Here it comes! Harder, harder," I yelped loudly.

"Urgghhh!!!" FB yelled.

We came together. I could feel the heat from his dick. It almost felt like we were fucking without a condom.

———

JAP

Damn! Why isn't she picking up da phone? Maybe she fell asleep. It is late, and she has been drinkin' all day. Maybe I should swerve by Trenice house and wake her up. I feel guilty as hell. I hope I don't show it. What if she can tell that I got some head?

Let me try again.

Still no answer.

Well, I can go home, take a shower, and rinse Destiny smell off of me. By dat time, I can decided what to do.

CHILL

She left no part of my body untouched or unlicked, from toes to forehead. Now, as I lie on my back, she's lying on top of me with her back to my chest. She had a foot on either side of my legs that she used to slide up and down my dick. One of my hands teased her nipples, while the other alternated between squeezing and rubbing her clit. She began movin' her hips in circles to R Kelly's "12 Play" CD. She pumped harder and harder as the groove caught her.

I knew she was close to the brink.

"Uh-uh... Not yet," I commanded in' her ear.

"Yes, it's coming. I'm ready," she answered back intensely.

I pulled out.

"Ooh, Chill! You a nasty nigga!"

"Dat's payback for da pool."

I grinned and swiftly flipped her on her stomach, while still inside her. I eased her legs closed and positioned mine on the outside of hers. I stroked up and down, left, right, 'round and 'round, to the "Bump 'n Grind" remix.

"Ahhh, baby, baby... I'm so in love with you," she cooed.

She closed her legs even tighter for more friction. "Just like I knew it would be," she chimed out, as she raised her ass, up and down, to meet my every thrust.

"Just like dat, sweetie. Give me all dat pussy."

"Take it, baby. You make me feel so good."

"Meet dat dick halfway, lift dat pussy, girl."

"Chill, this pussy yours... All yours."

"Yeah, baby. All mine," I replied, and turned us sideways. I lifted her top leg up and placed her foot on my thigh. I spit on two fingers, reached around, and massaged her clit.

132

"Ah...hh...hh! Shit! I'm finna nut on you dick."

"Let it out, baby. Don't hold it in. Let dat nut out."

"Yeah! Yeah!" She said excitedly, pushing herself harder into me.

I felt her muscles contract. She reached behind herself, gripped, and scratched my head. I used the same rhythm I was fuckin' her with to manipulate that clit. She gripped my dick like a hand was in her pussy. I was instantly jolted closer to nuttin'.

"Oh...fu...ck...gi...rl!" I shouted.

"Ooh...baby...ahh... I'm cum... I'm cum...ing!" she cried out in joy.

"Uhh-uhhh," I broke down behind her.

We lay that way for five minutes before she eased me out. She turned around and faced me. We lay on our sides, face to face.

"Baby?" Her breath was hot on my face.

"Yeah, sweetie?" I know I put it down. We had been sexin' for at least an hour. I figured I'd lay there for another fifteen, twenty minutes, so I don't make her feel bad. Then jump in the shower and head home to Lauren.

"You made good love to me," she complimented.

"Thank you, baby. But you brought dat out of me," I gave it right back.

She reached out and put a hand on my cheek, "But now I wanna see if you can fuck me good, too."

I never shy away from a challenge.

I slowly eased my face down between her legs.

"You betta hold on to da headboard or somethin', girl."

"Oh, it's like that?" she asked playfully.

"Oh yeah, it's just like dat!" I assured.

———

SHAY

"Trenice! Trenice!" I shouted into my phone, as I drove away from FB's house.

"What, girl? Stop yelling in my damn ear!" she shot back.

"Did Jap call or come by?"

"Nah, he supposed to? You said he might call. You ain't say come by."

"He was calling my phone and I didn't answer, so I figured he might have stopped by," I explained.

"I ain't heard from him, girl. Where you at now?"

"Headed to your house to clean up. If he calls or comes, tell him you sent me back to Walgreen's cause the stuff I bought you wasn't working and you're in a lot of pain and I left my phone there. You heard it ringing, but you're too hurt to get up."

"Shay, you need to stop your shit, chile! Jap is a good man. You shouldn't do him that way."

"Whatever, Tre. So you wanna know what went down tonight?"

"Uh, yeah. You gonna keep a bitch in suspense? Did Mr. Thang put it on you?"

I blushed and smiled, "Girl, let me tell you..."

———

"That bitch was super loose tonight," thought FB, as he lay back against his pillows and smoked a Newport. Now she finna go home and lay right up under her husband, triflin' bitch.

He laughed as his mind wandered to earlier, before Shay got to his crib. Wandered back to when he cut open the tips of all his condoms. He knew Shay wouldn't be paying close attention. She was drunk. He probably coulda hit raw, but nah... She wasn't that far gone. He nutted in her three times. She'd told FB that she hadn't been sleeping with her husband. That's why they'd been fuckin' more frequently. Shit, she'd even took a day or two off from work to come get dick down.

Nuthin'-ass hoe!

That's ok, I fixed her *and* her husband's ass tonight. The first step in the game had been taken. As Rouseau fell asleep, his only thoughts were:

"Welcome to the world of AIDS hoe.

Welcome to the world of AIDS."

———

JAP

I can't get this feelin' of guilt from inside me. I feel like I let Jr. down. Would I feel better if I told Shay the deal? Nah… She'd really leave me then. I wanna talk to somebody, but I know Chill and M1 probably think I'm stupid. Shit, maybe I am stupid. One of da finest video girls out there just took her mouth off my dick. Niggas be fantasizin' 'bout dis bitch and here I am feelin' bad for myself. It's 3:40 in the morn.

"Come on, Shay, where you at?"

I reached to call her cell phone again, but you know what? Maybe it's good she ain't here yet. I think I'm too guilty to be around her.

<Ring Ring>

Speakin' of da devil.

"What's up, baby?"

"I'm sorry I missed your call, baby."

"Where you at?"

"On my way back to Tre's house. I had to go back to Walgreen's 'cause the medicine I brought her wasn't helping. So I got her something else. She's in a lot of pain. She might have to go to the hopsital."

"Dat's fucked up. I hope she feels better. You gonna stay da night wit' her?"

"I wasn't planning on it. But maybe I need to. In case she has to go to the emergency room. She's been throwing up too."

"I feel you, baby."

"Are you ok? You sound strange. Do you need me to come home?"

"Nah… Take care of ya homegirl. She needs you. I'm good."

"You sure?"

"Yeah, I'm straight."

"Ok, baby. I love you."

"I love you too, Shay."

We hung up.

————

CHILL

"Dis what you want?" I asked her.

"Umm, damn...right, baby!"

"I can't hear you. You playin'. I'm finna take dis dick out."

She was standing spread eagle, like she was getting' frisked by the police, against the full length mirror of the bedroom closet door. . I had one hand pulling her hair back against me and the other holding one of her legs in the air.

"You better not! Don't try that shit again."

I rammed her ass, hard and decent.

"You... talk... dat... shit... now... bitch!" I challenged, through clenched teeth.

I'm hittin' her wit' dat Henny dick.

"Ahh... I'm sor... ooo, ooo, ooo, ooo."

"Bitch, did I say talk?" I growled.

I snatched her, tossed her on the bed, back down, and pushed her knees up to either side of her ears, in da buck.

She got bold, "That's all you working with?" she taunted wit' a smirk.

I raised my eyebrow and slammed off in her. I had her laid down on the edge of da bed wit' my feet planted firmly on da carpet for leverage.

"Ok, ok, ok, oh shit, my pus..."

"Yo' pussy what? Huh?"

"My...uh...What you doing to me, baby?"

She reached down and started strokin' herself. She was using her hips to bounce back at me.

"Come on, gimme my dick! It's mine! All mine!"

"Yeaah... Dis you dick. Now come and get it."

"Mine, yeah! Mine, yeah!" she humped faster and faster. She grabbed my neck to pull me down, licked my lips, then sucked my bottom lip.

I felt myself about to give away. I pulled out and nutted all over her stomach and titties.

"Ahhhhh," I growled.

"I'm cummin', Chill, I'm cummin', you...nut...hot... ssss, uhhh..." She started shakin' like a leaf.

I let her legs go and collapsed on top of her. She lifted my head up and held my face with both hands. She was smilin'.

"I love you, Chill. I really do." "I feel you, l'il momma," I said, and rolled off of her. I was fuckin' exhausted. I just needed to rest my eyes for ten minutes. Then I would take a shower and go home.

———

The candles burned slowly, with the scent of jasmine. Keith Sweat was pouring out the speakers embedded in the ceiling, and Lauren lay relaxed and oiled down in her lingerie, from Frederick's of Hollywood. She'd put red satin on the bed, from her overnight bag. Now all that was missing was Mante'.

"Please come home soon, Mante'," she exhaled and whispered to herself. "I'm waiting for you, baby." She closed her eyes and fantasized.

The clock on the wall read 4:45 a.m. It was getting later and later, but she still held on to hope.

The hope that Mante' wouldn't let her down.

"Mante', you promised," she said to herself, as she took another sip of champagne and waited.

———

CHILL

When I woke up, I was under a blanket with Poca snuggled up close to me and birds were chirping. My throat and mouth were dry and my head was foggy. I could see the early morning sunshine through the thin curtains. I rubbed my eyes to gain some focus.

Got – damn!

I sat up quick, too quick, on the side of the bed, with my elbows on my knees and hands on the sides of my head. I stood at the window, wishing I could make the sun go back down and reverse time.

Fuck!

BRANDON Q. HEPBURN

I took a quick shower and went to find M1. I didn't have any of my whips there. I had ridden wit' Jap. Plus, I didn't feel like driving. I found him in one of the rooms, in the middle of the bed between Selena, Mya, and Talia. Everyone was butt-ass naked. I pulled his leg, and he opened an eye.

"Man, get up. Put some clothes on and shoot me by da crib."

"Um, hm," he moaned and turned on his side, resting his face on Mya's breast.

I pulled his leg again, "Get up, fool! Get dressed. I need you to take me to da crib."

"Damn, my nigga. You'll fuck up a wet dream. You see a nigga laid between all these model lookin' bitches and you come and wake a nigga up. You a hater!" He sat up, trying to catch his bearings. "I'm gettin' up, my nigga."

Ten minutes later, he came down on wobbly legs.

"How long dis gonna take? 'Cause I'm coming right back here. I heard dat pill shit last twelve hours or some shit. Nigga, dem hoes was poppin' two or three beans at a time. I know dey got another couple hours of get loose in' dey system. Shiit, I'm trying to capitalize."

"Damn, pussy gotta nigga using big words early in the mornin', huh?" I teased my nigga.

"I'm sayin', doe. Why you don't just take da whip?"

"I need some company, fool. I fucked up."

He looked at me, "I know you fucked up. You still here. Nigga, I told you stupid-ass to go home!" He shook his head, "All dat holsum-ass pussy gone to waste."

We headed out da door.

I shook my head, too, "I was on my way, and then Poca... And, boy, we fucked around and got loose."

"Fuckin' wit' my cousin', you wasn't on your way no where, fool."

On da way there he told me what went down some hours ago.

"Nigga, you ain't hearin' what I'm saying. I fucked eight hoes last night!" He looked over at me. "For free, nigga!" He cocked his head to da side, "Fool, dat's like a world record or somethin', ain't it?"

The nigga had me laughin'.

"Y'all niggas was loose!" I dapped him up.

138

"Yeah, you know dem young niggas ain't ever got down like dat. But dey handled dat, though."

"Even *I* ain't had eight before. I think my most is four."

"You know what I did, right?" He smiled showing all his gold teeth.

"What you did, fool?" I started smiling too. I knew he was finna say somethin' stupid.

"When we first got started, I went 'round and gave each hoe three pumps. Dat way, if I ran outta gas I could still say I fucked all dem bitches, nigga!"

I bust out laughin', "Boy, you a gotdamn fool!" My gotdamn stomach hurt.

My dawg had lifted my spirits without even tryin', but dat feeling quickly evaporated when we pulled up to my house and Lauren's car wasn't there.

I felt low.

I ain't wanna show how hurt I felt, so I said, "Let me grab a change of clothes. I'm a fall back 'round there wit' you. Shit, we might as well have they asses cook breakfast for da boys," I said, knowing all I really wanted was to make shit scraight with Lauren.

I made it to my bedroom. I looked around. I saw the satin sheets and snubbed out candles and smelled the lingering scent of Lauren's body. I felt ten times worse. I saw a note in the middle of the bed:

Dear Mante',

I can endure what most others can't, and I can stick by when most others fall by the wayside. All I asked for in return was your honesty and respect. That's all. I don't ask you to be perfect, and I don't ask you to change. You looked me in the eyes and gave me your word, Mante'. A word that, once upon a time, I could count on and trust without hesitation. But some things change and people do too. I hope it was worth it. I hope it was worth me.

Yours Truly,
Not meant to be

I sat down on the edge of the bed. I could've call her. I should've call her. But for once in my life, I didn't know if I had the right words to say. And I also knew not to rush it. She needed time to cool off, and that was understandable. I know I hurt her – badly. So I had to play to her tune, not mine.

I jumped back in the whip with M1. I guess he could read my silence or the expression on my face – take your pick.

He glanced over, "You straight, fool?" He asked sincerely.

"Yeah, I'm good, dawg." I responded, in a subdued manner.

"Look, dawg… It ain't no secret. I know how you feel about Lauren. And I know last night you 'posed to do ya thang. I feel bad my cousin fucked dat up for you."

"Can't blame her. It ain't her fault; it's mine. You know Poca a dime piece herself. I just got caught thinkin' with my dick."

"I dig it, my nigga. If it was me, and she wasn't family, I wouldn't got caught slippin' too. Da bitch is bad."

"So I'm a just give her time to cool off. Then I'll just give it to her raw and admit I did some foul shit."

"Shit gonna be straight, fool. But what you gonna do 'bout Poca? You know she vibin' you on some wifey-type shit."

"You know what? She kept tellin' me she love me, while we was fuckin'. But I thought dat was them beans talking. So I ain't even sweat it, but now dat you mention it."

"She been asking 'bout ya relationship status and what not since she been here. Plus, I heard her l'il homegirls whisperin' some shit bout you. I know how she get. Shit, you know too. You know dat muhfucka persistent as fuck." He looked over at me.

"I know, but I ain't gonna play wit' her, though. I've known her too long and respect her and you too much for dat. So I'm a just be real wit' her. Let her know I ain't on dat wifey shit wit' her."

"She gonna take dat shit ta heart. She can't stand rejection. Shiit, I don't think she eva been rejected," he acknowledged.

"Yeah, but I gotta handle it like dat. Any other way gonna be too much conflict. We got big business we handlin' together. I can't drag her like I do dem l'il broads in da street, ya feel me?. I don't need her all sour at a nigga, at a time like dis, especially!"

"Oh, I know my nigga. I'm just statin' da facts. But you know when you took it there, you mixed business with pleasure. Not sayin' dat you can't, 'cause it ain't *what* you do, it's *how*. But you woulda been betta off hittin' one of da otha hoes. Know what I'm sayin'? Less strings attached."

"You right. But it's done now, so…" I said, as we pulled up in the driveway. I gotta handle dat asap."

"Cous' ain't gonna lay down so easy," he noted, over the roof of the whip. "She ain't eva been a quitta," he spoke seriously.

CHAPTER 24

JAP/SHAY/CHILL

"Hey, baby," I greeted groggily, as Shay climbed into da bed next to me.

"Morning," she said back.

"How Trenice doin'? Do she feel betta?" I inquired.

"The medicine I gave her the second time seemed to work. She was in less pain, and it put her to sleep, finally. I'll check on her in a couple of hours. Right now, I'm so tired, I just want to sleep."

"I feel you, baby." I scooted up on her, in da spoon position. I wrapped my arms around her and snuggled. Now that I was fully awake, my mind instantly went back to what happened in da wee hours of dis mornin'. But I decided it's best to keep my mouth shut. We have enough problems to deal wit', wit'out addin' mo' drama. I just have to learn to deal wit' da guilt and hope dat, one day, it'll leave.

Layin' here next to my wife felt good 'cause we haven't done so in a minute. It was turnin' me on to feel Shay's warm, familiar body next to me. I got hard instantly. It's been so long since we had any sexual contact. Shiit, I'm tired of jackin' my dick!

I closed my arms around her tighter, pulled her closer, and started grindin' my dick on her. I was waitin' on her to push back up on me, but I was gettin' no response. So, I grinded a l'il harder and started playin' with her nipples.

She moved my hand.

"Uh, uh... I'm tired, Jap."

"I know, baby." I kissed da back of her neck, "I just want to feel you. Just let me stick it in, you ain't gotta do nothin'," I persuaded.

142

"I'm not in da mood, Jap. I'm tired and my head hurts from taking care of my sick friend all night. I don't feel like having sex." Wit' dat, she rolled away from me and lay on her stomach.

I lay on my back, put my arm across my forehead, and exhaled a deep, frustrated breath. Man, I'm so sick of dis shit. It's been about a month and she still wit' dis fuck shit.

Man...something has to give!

"Shay, I need to tell you somethin'," I continued lookin'

248

at da ceilin'.

No response?

I blurted it out.

SHAY

If this nigga only knew how sore and worn out all three of my holes are. If I would've known that he was gonna crack for some ass, I would've stayed at Tre's house. I just wanna sleep and let my body get back to normal. Besides, if he really wanted some pussy, he'd take it. But he wants ta be with that love dovey, passive shit.

Hold up!

Did I hear right?

Did this muthafucker just say he got his dick sucked last night? And he should've fucked too?

My eyes popped open.

JAP

I couldn't control myself. All my frustration finally got da best of me. To da point that I didn't give a fuck what happened next. I told her and sat on da edge of da bed.

"What did you just say, Jap?" Shay questioned sternly.

"I said, last night I got some head. I don't have any excuses to give you. Shit happens, my bad." I explained nonchalantly.

She sat up in da bed, pulled da alarm clock out da socket, and threw it at me. It grazed my head.

"Shit happens! Muthafucka, what the fuck do you mean, shit happens? What, you slipped and fell and your dick landed in a bitch mouth? She got up out da bed. "What bitch was it, Jap? The same bitch who grabbed your ass, huh?"

She was up in my face when I responded, "Actually, I got drunk and high, on top of no pussy for a month, and my dick ended up in a bitch mouth! And it don't matter who da fuck it was," I ended sarcastically.

Bap!

She swung on me.

She tried to hit me again. I don't beat up on women, but I restrained her and pushed her on da bed.

"Shay, don't put you hands on me no mo'," I told her seriously.

"Or what? Huh? Fuck you, Jap! Fuck you!" She stood back up.

"I ain't sayin' dat it makes it right. But fuck what you think. Dat was da first and only time. So you been round her starvin' a nigga for pussy over nothin'. 'Cause da way I feel now, if I had been beatin' somethin' else, I'd damn sho tell you ass!" I'm hot as fuck. I'm sick of dis shit.

"Fuck you, Jap, and your dirty-ass dick!" she shouted, as she stood up.

"Naw... Fuck you, Shay. A nigga round here caterin' to you ass... You don't want for shit – financially, mentally, or emotionally. I make sure you straight, I break my neck fo' you ass. And you got da nerve to tell me I can't get no pussy. You my muhfuckin' wife!" I had never went off like dis. Chill woulda been proud of me.

"No, I *was* your muthafuckin' wife! Before you decided to stick your dick in another bitch mouth. I –"

"You what, Shay? I know I'm wrong, so it's nothin' you can say. So you what? You wanna leave me? What? I tell you what, you ain't got to, 'cause I'll holla!" I slipped on some 'drobe and hit it.

SHAY

I've got to be losing my damn mind! My husband just sat up here and told me he let another bitch suck his dick. He has never talked to me like that. What the fuck! Did he just get bold overnight or some shit? I could say, "Shay, you brought this on yourself. What goes around...yada, yada, yada." But, fuck that! I was only protecting myself. And from the looks of things, I did the right muthafuckin' thing. I don't care what he says. Whether or not I gave his ass pussy, he would've cheated. What if I was sick or had surgery, and couldn't have sex – then what? Just like my damn daddy. He ain't no different.

But I gotta trick for that ass!

I'll show him how to be hoeish.

———

JAP

"What's up, fool?" I said, as Chill answered his pipe.

"Ain't nothin'... What dey do?"

"Hey, you still 'round da way or you at da crib?"

"I'm still in da same spot. Me and M1 just put they ass to work cookin' breakfast. Why? What up?" he asked.

"I'm finna swing through. I'll holla at you when I get there."

"Fa sho.'"

When I got there, all da girls were walkin' around in skimpy, boy-shorts and wifebeaters. A few ain't have on nothin'.

"Just what I need," I thought sarcastically.

"Hey, Jap!" Destiny greeted me wit' a hug and smile.

"What dey do, sweetie?" I hollered back.

Her, Poca, and Heaven were in da kitchen doin' they thing on da stove.

"I hope y'all know what y'all doing, 'cause I'm hungry as fuck."

"Negro, please! We are country girls," Heaven explained. "We was cookin' in our mammy coochie!"

"Dat shit sound good. But you can fry ice cream wit' ya mouthpiece."

"No booboo, I actually fry mine in a skillet," retorted Destiny.

I looked at her skeptically, "Whateva... Where da fellas at?" I questioned.

"They're out there in the backyard, waiting on us to finish and serve them," replied Poca.

L'il Bit walked, in, "They think they some kings or some shit. Talkin' 'bout breakfast by the pool. Chile, please," she added sarcastically.

"We *are* kings. You just make sure you ass is polite when you serve a nigga or you ain't getting tipped."

"Nigga, tip ya tongue on this pussy. How 'bout that?" The girls giggled.

"Dat's alright, though. I know my l'il homeboy put it on you ass while you talkin'," I joked.

She blushed, "He was alright. He wasn't all dat," she smiled, "He did a l'il somethin', somethin'."

"Good enough to have you ghetto-ass grocery shoppin' an' shit." I eyed the Publix bags in her hands.

"Fuck... you!" She laughed.

"Speak for yo'self, girl. Shawty, got a dick like a mule," admitted Selena.

"Nah, you just gotta l'il girl coochie," teased L'il Bit.

"It keep your mouth full!" Selena shot back.

"Y'all shot out, but y'all need to hurry up wit' dat grub," I said, and headed out da kitchen side-door.

"What dey do, Big Jap?" M1 called out when he saw me comin'.

"What up, Jap? What up?" greeted Chaunce and Goon.

I dapped up everybody.

"Shay must still be wit' Trenice or somethin'. Two days in a row, you out da house. You betta stop befo' niggas start thinkin' you got a life an' shit," Chill kidded.

"Fuck Shay! I don't give a fuck where she at!" I exclaimed angrily.

M1 and Chill looked at each other.

"Uh oh... What happened now?" M1 questioned.

I explained me and Shay conversation dat mornin'.

"My nigga, I got so heated I just spit da shit out. I just told her," I continued, "Thing was, dat I didn't give a fuck what she thought. It was like, 'whateva'."

"See, dat's what I'm talkin' 'bout, my nigga. Dat's how you man up." M1 amped up like he was pushin' four fifteens.

"Only thing I'm worried bout is Jr. 'cause I really don't know where me and Shay goin' from here. I just hope dis don't fuck up his life." CHILL

I was listening to Jap, but I was quietly contemplating. M1 kept glancing at me. He probably was thinking the same thing as me. I could tell some guilt was starting to seep in on Jap. That's why he brought up his son. I knew later on it would hit him like a ton of coke. And, although I told myself I would sleep on things for a couple of days, I'm not comfortable letting my homeboy run guilt trips on herself for nothin'.

I gotta tell 'em.

"Hey, Chaunce, Goon, y'all go check on da girls for a minute. Give us a l'il privacy."

M1 knew what time it was.

"Yeah, y'all niggas break off. Dis grown folk shit." One added his two cents.

When they walked off, I took a swig of the mimosa (orange juice and champagne) I was drinking.

I took a deep breath.

"Fool, I need to tell you somethin'," I started off. "It's about Shay," I waited for his response.

"Chill, I don't like da sound of dat. Watchin' your body language, I know dis finna be some real creep shit. Dawg, just tell me." He eyed me.

"I found out yesterday. I don't even know if I was gonna tell you. I told myself dat I'd sleep on it. I didn't wanna be wrong. But wit' da shit dat's happenin' now, knowing you gonna be eventually feelin' shitty, probably fa no reason, I gotta tell you."

M1 just listened in silence as Jap braced himself for the worst.

"What you mean for no reason, fool? My nigga, tell me, dawg!" he demanded.

"Fool, Lauren..." I ran the whole play down to him. When I finished, my nigga looked like all the life had been sucked out of him. He looked over at M1 and then back at me.

"Why y'all ain't tell me yesterday? What you mean you don't know if you was gonna tell me or not?" he asked. "My nigga, she ain't just fucking round, she pissin' on niggas and shit!"

"Dawg... Number one: we ain't wanna be wrong. Two: a nigga know how you feel ya wifey. So we ain't even know if you'd belive us or not. We ain't want you sour at us, fool," One explained.

"Yeah, I know how I am 'bout her, too. But at da same time, I know Lauren ain't gonna make up no shit like dis. Dawg, my wife is givin' niggas golden showers. Ain't no tellin' what otha looseness she into," he shook his head. "I gotta handle dis, I got to. I'm finna go back to da house and make her straighten me. Real shit! I played succa boy for too long." He made to get up.

"Hold up, fool. You emotional right now. You go back home now, and you might beat her ass and go to jail. I got a better idea 'cause I know common sense tellin' you it's tue, but ya heart still need proof. So dis what we gonna do. When she go to work tomorrow, you're gonna go to da crib, snatch her spare remote and car key, go to the dealer, and get a third copy of both. Dat's gravy 'cause both y'all name on da whip. Next, we gonna hit da Spy Shop and grab a couple of items."

"The first is a GPS tracker. They sell you a l'il bug dat you stick on ya car, in or out. It comes wit' a l'il handheld screen, about da size of a Gameboy. Wherever she goes, it'll show on da screen. Next, we gonna grab a twenty-four-hour voice-activated recorder. Whenever someone in dat car start talkin', it's recordin'. It blocks out radio frequency, so we won't have no unnecessary gibberish to listen to. What y'all think?"

Jap nodded his head while he mulled it over.

"Hell! Fuck yeah!" M1 called out. Dat Spy Shop is da shit. Dat's how I caught dat nigga Head. Jap boy, like G-shit, fool."

"I'm wit' it. But don't think I don't believe y'all. But you right, Chill, ain't nothin' like seein' and hearin' for yo'self. Shit, I wanna do dat shit right now," he answered.

"Just take it easy, dawg. Lamp da rest of da day and tomorrow we'll put it down."

Right then, four beautiful looking ladies came out carrying an even more beautiful looking breakfast.

It was time to eat.

―――――

"I love him, I do," thought Lauren. "I love Mante' with all my heart. He's my one true love. I thought that I could wait, but after last night, imagining him with another woman, I'm starting to question whether we will ever be together. My heart tells me he loves me, but my mind is taking over. It's five in in' the afternoon. Why am I still crying? He hasn't even called to check on me. If he's supposed to be such a womanizer, then he'd know that I probably wouldn't answer his calls. But just seeing his number would let me know that he cares or at least that he's thinking of me."

"I miss him already, but I can't do this any longer. I have my own life to live. I don't want to hurt anymore. I have to separate myself from Mante'. I just need...time," Lauren thought, as she cried herself back to sleep.

CHAPTER 25

SUNDAY NIGHT
ROU

I know it's a million niggas out there who had fucked up lives and mine ain't no different. I been to hell and back only to fight my way out, just to have hell living within me. I could forever question God... why... But I'm past that. As I sit here staring at a blank TV screen, I know the only person that I should forever question is myself, for making the choices that put me in this predicament – the choices that force me to live with the devil's disease.

Two and a half years ago, I was normal. I mean normal by a nigga's standards anyway. I was gettin' money, had a bad l'il wifey, and was fuckin' a bunch of females – one who just happened to be my wife's sister, Shamira. See, normal by a street nigga's standards. Me and Shamira started fucking regularly. I was thirty-seven, she was thirty-five, five years older than Jasmine, my girl. Shamira was bad, I couldn't resist. Shiit, she still bad, 5'5", black as the Marianna's Trench, pink lips, and eyes that change from gray to green. She kept her hair cut short, and she was hairy. She had an ass that shook like tremors from an earthquake when she walked. I guess "exotic" is one good word to describe her and "freaky" is another.

Just like a nigga, I was fucking Shamira raw, but that wasn't the problem. The problem was that my girl somehow found out about our little secret. Instead of confronting us about it, she used it as an excuse to justify fucking this nigga who she already wanted to fuck. At first, she held off 'cause she was faithful. The nigga name was Tank. He was a high-level paper chaser with a spot on the Bab (Ali Baba Ave.) in Opa Locka. All the honeys were on his jock, and my girl was no different. She was looking for an excuse to fuck the nigga, and it just so happen that he was her best friend's cousin – easy access.

She started fucking dude raw, was still fucking me raw, and I was fucking Shamira raw. The nigga gave her that ninja (AIDS), and she passed it to me, and I gave it to her sister. Then, on top of that, when Jasmine found out, she blamed me and her sister, then killed herself. She ain't do like most women, with pills or slitting her wrist. This bitch shot herself in the head with my chrome .357 Magnum. Nobody knows whatever happened to Tank, but I heard he gave that shit to over fifty females.

That left just me and Mira. Of course, we were pissed. But we were guilty for what we were doing. Eventually, we did what we had to do, and that's deal with it. Having this shit will teach you one thing though – and that's how to hustle. 'Cause if yo' ass ain't got the money to buy the latest and best drugs, you're a dead muthafucka.

Shamira still does her thing. She strips, hustles, and fucks for money. Nobody knows that she has the disease. Matter fact, don't nobody know *I* got shit. Everybody thinks Jasmine killed herself over my hoeish ways. Only her and her best friend knew about her and Tank. They really kept it on the low being the fact that I'm in the streets and well-known, too. Nobody knows the whole secret of our little devil's diamond.

This damn disease fucks up your whole frame of mind. You feel like the worlds owes you and you wanna take all you can from it. It turned Mira all the way out. She strips and tricks for cash, but it's more *where* the money comes from that matters. Niggas! Her mission is to make niggas pay for the disease that, whether she accepted it or not, came from a nigga. In her mind, if the money that she uses for her meds and treatment comes from dudes, then ultimately they're paying, no matter how indirectly. She gets satisfaction from that, where she can't get satisfaction out of life. That's why I need her for the third part in my plan. The second part is M1, and that's handled.

Just like Mira got it from a nigga, for the right price, I hope she'll be willing to give it to a nigga.

<Ring Ring Ring>

Who the fuck is this interrupting my thoughts?

Well, what do we have here?

"Hello?" I answered to none other than Shay herself.

"What's up, boo? What are you doing?" she asked.

"Ain't nothing, just sitting here flipping through channels. What's going on with you?" I wondered, "I didn't expect to hear from you for at least a week or two."

"Surprise, surprise, then. You never know what kind of gifts you may receive suddenly and unexpectedly," she chanted.

I chuckled. "Yeah, you sure are right 'bout that." I almost felt a little bit of guilt. "Does that mean this gift may show up at my house, or do I just get to hear it's voice?" I said.

"I don't know… It's your gift. You tell it what to do," she responded slyly.

"Well, in that case, I want my gift wrapped in the sluttiest thing she can find. And I want it delivered on its knees with its mouth open."

"Umm, I believe that can be managed. We have a twenty-four-hour delivery service, also. So, I can have that package slut-wrapped and delivered in about two hours, say 11 o'clock. Is that good?"

"Yeah, that's on point. I'll be waiting."

"Good. Ciao!" She hung up.

That bitch knows she can role play. That shit makes my dick hard instantly. I don't know what my cousin doing… Whatever it is, it's not enough. I knew when he first met her that he couldn't handle her. Don't matter now anyway. It's a shame all that good pussy gotta go to waste. Oh, well, that's life. She can blame her husband and his homeboys for that. Shiit… They made it this way.

It's a good sign she's coming back tonight. After this, I won't fuck with her no more. Might as well hit it one time for ol' time sake and a little bit of insurance. Then, when she try to hit me up again, I'll tell her we can't do this anymore, I feel bad for Jap or some shit. Shay kinda fucked up in the head. I hope she don't be wit' dat stalking and shit. I gotta separate myself from her. With a little bit of luck, when I break off, she'll start hitting somebody else and won't even suspect I'm the one gave it to her. If not, it don't matter. I'm getting missing soon anyway.

In the meantime, I need to make a call to Shamira, see if she wants to make a little bit of change.

CHAPTER 26

TUESDAY, AUGUST 11
CHILL

Peep this shit. This shit is sweeter than I thought. I'm talkin' sweeter than bare pussy! Ya dig. We're on the way to the girls hideout. We just finished pickin' up the first days worth of cash that we dropped yesterday. With our insides, everything cleared today. We working on ten accounts this week, ten next week, ten every week, openin' up ten accounts every week. That way, when ten accounts are ready to drop one week, another ten will be ready the next week.

We dropped between four and five stacks on each account everyday. Right now I got on me between forty and fifty grand – one day. I don't like to count my cash before it come, but our projected income by Thursday, which should be the last day, is somewhere between one twenty and one hundred fifty thousand. We're paying each girl five stacks each account or five stacks a week, however you want to look at it.

Me, Jap, Ev, and Kat bust down the rest.

Once we got to the house, me and Jap broke off in one of the rooms solo and got the chips right.

"Dis is what I'm talkin' 'bout, boy. We shoulda been had dis shit jumpin' like dis!" exclaimed an excited Jap.

"I know. I been said we needed an inside. Plus, the IDs make it even sweeter."

"So how long do you think it's gonna last 'fo dey hit Evelyn and Kathleen up?" he inquired.

"I been wonderin' myself, tryin' to estimate a little. I mean things we have in our favor, thus far, are the fact that we opened up accounts at a bunch of different branches, not just with Evelyn. So it ain't too much heat on her. Only thing, she's branch manager, so anything that fucks up in the bank makes her look bad, feel me?

As for Kat, just the fact that she is head teller is heat itself. The fact that she doesn't necessarily clear the checks and release the funds is a plus. But she authorizes the clearin'. So the higher ups could start to question her judgment real quick. I'm thinkin' she'll be lucky to make it more than three months escapin' suspicion, and that's pushin' it. Unless –"

"Unless what, fool? I can tell when you came up wit' somethin'."

"Ok, listen. They don't do any kind of photo imagery when we start the accounts, right." I said more of a statement than a question.

"So, from now on, when we send the girls in, they gonna be crackas," I looked at him.

He looked perplexed when he asked, "Crackas?"

"We gonna have Poca and da girls put da makeup game down, wit' da elegant attire to match, so we can pass da girls off as rich, white people. That does two things. One, it'll stop the tellers from asking Kat's permission all da time on whether to clear checks or release money. Plus, when it hits corporate investigations, Kat won't look so bad clearin' checks for supposedly rich white folk, as she would wit' blacks. And on top of dat, we're gonna make Kat put a hold on a couple of checks and freeze a couple of accounts on da girls, but while they're in their black personas."

He nodded his head, "I wish we woulda been thought of dat. We coulda had 'em open up da accounts as crackas from da get-go.

"Yeah, but hindsight got 20/20 vision," I acknowledged.

"I feel you. Dat plan is tightwork. We just have to make sure dey makeup game is on point."

"You been seein' da same shit I have. Poca and Heav and 'em could be workin' in somebody movie studio. Shit, they learned in da same school as them muthafuckas. If I didn't know 'em personally when they in disguise, I wouldn't recognize 'em. So now we need to break it down to them, Kat and Ev."

154

"Everybody gonna agree. You know anything 'bout savin' a bitch ass they all for it."

"You gotta pick up Jr., right?"

He looked at his watch, "Yeah, I got 'bout an hour befo' I hit."

"Dis shit still seem strange to me. It's been over a month. I ain't seen you dis much in years."

"Just like back in da day, huh?" he smiled.

"Yeah, but I wish it was unda better circumstances. I mean we gettin' money, but I know you hurtin', dawg. I feel ya pain, my nigga."

We had Shay under constant surveillance with the equipment we picked up from the Spy Shop. We had heard a lot of conversations with her and other niggas. We heard and saw her hollerin' at niggas at the car wash, stores, even at the red light. We heard her goin' off on some nigga answerin' machine who ain't been answerin' her calls. She obviously was fuckin' buddy 'cause in her rantin' and ravin', she said as much.

We also crept on her at a couple niggas' houses late night. We GPSed her to a couple of eat-in restaurants, out with niggas and shit. L'il momma been super loose. But through it all, my dawg been takin' it like a G. I know fool done shed some tears in da dark, and I feel 'em. I ain't ever felt for a woman like that, maybe except for Lauren. And I doubt if it can measure up to being married and having your only shorty from the girl. I probably would cry too. I'm a spiteful-ass nigga, so I woulda done worse, found some type of way to get getback.

I ain't brought up the issue, but da nigga ain't put in for a divorce. So I know he still loves her 'cause he tryin' to hold on to lost love.

He looked down at the floor, "It's been hell, Chill. Watchin' someone you spent every night wit' fo' almost three years, been wit' even longer, doin' her thang like she ain't got a husband – like I don't exist. But what's worse, my nigga, dawg, dis between me and you."

"Don't try no nigga, man. You know what time it is."

"I know how M1 is, and I don't want him fuckin' wit' me," I nodded my head, "'Cause he don't understand."

"You don't give fool enough credit, but I feel you," I told 'em.

"But what's worse is dat I'm still holdin' on, hopin' dat shit would somehow turn around for us. How flaw is dat?"

Yeah, dat was pretty flaw, but what I said was, "Dat's your wife and your jit momma. You'd be wrong not to feel somethin', even if just for Jr.'s sake. I mean like you said, this is somebody who you spent years outta your life wit'. Those feelin's ain't gonna go away overnight and you can't turn 'em on and off like a light switch. Yet, you gotta use some kind of common sense."

"I know, dawg, I know. I been prolongin' dis divorce shit, but I know it gotta be done."

"Shit, wit' all da shit we got on her, she'll have hell winnin' a custody battle, female or not."

"Yeah, I hollered at Lauren, and she put me down wit' a mean lawyer. 'Cause I gotta take it there. I can't have my son around all dem niggas and shit. He might fuck 'round and be confused or some shit. And if she ain't givin' a fuck 'bout herself, ain't no tellin', she might take shit out on him, tryin' to get at me. I ain't gonna put my shorty in dat predicament." All I heard was Lauren's name.

"When I go pick jit up or drop jit off, she act like she ain't got no rap for a nigga. But, shit… I play it da same way. Even though I know like hell I wanna talk to her. But I know dat's what she want, and I'm tired of playin' da flaw role. She stay tryin' to tempt a nigga, too. Wearin' l'il or nothin', or tight and skimpy. You ever wanted somebody bad as fuck but at the same time dey disgust you?. It's like, I love dis muhfucka so much, my nigga, but I don't like her ass!" he confided.

"You know I ain't eva really been deep in no shit like dat, but I can imagine just by goin' off your vibe. I'm sayin, though, you ain't tell me you talked to Lauren," I said, changin' the subject.

"My bad, fool. Dat was like three weeks ago. When I first started findin' out all dis shit Shay was doin', when I got missin' for dem few days," he explained.

"Yeah, I wish she'd answer my calls."

"I know, dawg… She'll come round. I tried to bring dat shit up, but she wasn't having it. She told me if I continued to talk about you she would end da phone call. Dat's probably why I didn't tell you I spoke to her. I 'on't like tellin' you no shit like dat."

"Damn, she hate a nigga like dat? Man, I send flowers, singin' telegrams, wine, bread, and cheese, everyday. I been doin' dis shit for 'bout a month. Everyday she get somethin' delivered to her, and she still won't holla at me. She even sent her assistant to drop off my monthly financial report, like she don't even want me comin' to the office. I ain't ever chased after no chick like dis, seekin' her forgiveness. Honestly, I'm startin' to get aggravated," I admitted.

"You know what da ol' coons say. Dat da ones you gotta wait and struggle fo', dem be da ones dat you hold on to."

"I hear you!" I said sarcastically. "Then I still got Poca breathin' down my muhfuckin' neck. I gave it to her raw and uncut, but she still ain't tryin' to let a nigga loose. She on some 'she got patience, good things come to those who wait' type shit. I'm like, 'L'il momma, you need to ease up. Let's keep handlin' dis business and dead dat other shit'."

"You only hit dat one time, right?" he questioned.

"Man, I only hit dat one night, dawg." He looked at me skeptically, with his mouth pushed to da side. I smiled, "Nah... I ain't gonna lie. I hit one mo' time. But it was supposed to be, you know, like a no-hard-feelin's fuck or somethin'. Yeah, I wanted to smash, 'cause Poca on dat freaky shit. I love dat shit. Boy, you just dont' know!" I shook my head. "But it was a one last fuck thing."

"I hear you, but dat last fuck probably made her see some light at da end of da tunnel."

"Yeah, I know... Send mixed signals an shit. I already know. I'm a vet, nigga. I knew it before I screwed it, but I ain't give a fuck. I knocked her loose anyway. Since then. I been keepin' her at a distance. But check you out. You been airin' Destiny out every chance you get."

He grinned, "But I told her what time it is. I ain't tryin' to jump in nothin' serious. She wit' dat. She on some 'have fun while it last' type shit. We just enjoyin' da moment. Besides, da other night' I had her, Heaven and Talia. So don't get it twisted, nigga!" he nodded his head with an arrogant grin.

It was good to see my dawg smile, even if only temporarily. You gotta start somewhere. And I know when he get through this shit, whether sooner or later, my dawg gonna find real joy.

I gave my nigga dap.

"Well, you ain't da only one been loose, fool. I done ran through da bunch of dem myself, repeatedly. So much for not mixin' business wit' pleasure, huh?" I joked.

"Wit' our line of work, our business has always been pleasure and our pleasure always business. Well, at least, on you end, up until recently. So, yeah, I respect dat rule. But whoever made it need to respect our hustle. 'Cause they obviously didn't have da benefit of havin' pussy attached to dey grind, before, and not after da come-up. Ya feel me?" I nodded my head listenin'. "Keep it real. We surrounded by ten bad-ass females, on a daily basis. Bitches who a nigga will pay a stack or betta to run up in. You already know how Poca and L'il Bit tax game is. So it a be a different story if I was still into my marriage. But I 'on't know any nigga dat would have a layout like dis and ain't sample da goods. Fuck sample! Niggas would try to have a full course meal!. Maybe, and I say *maybe*, except Hugh Hefner ol' pimped-out ass. Shiit… I think even he done damn near ran through all da Playboy girls. Dat Viagra-ass muhfucka. Niggas selling dat shit like they Ecstasy or some shit. Dis last month, I realized I been missin' out on da action all dis time. I mean, I knew what it is, but I been chillin' for so long I got numb to da shit. Nigga, ain't no mo' black rock on my dick!" He nodded his head, "Boy, it's going down. You hear dat Chill? It's goin' down!"

"I hear you, dawg. I hear you," I acknowledged.

He looked at his watch, "Let me go pick jit up. I'm a fuck wit' you later."

"Aight, I holla," I shot back.

We dapped up and left out da room.

CHAPTER 27

WEDNESDAY, AUGUST 12, 9:17 P.M.
ROU

"What's up, bruh?" Shamira greeted, as she came into my office.

I told her to come 'round dis time 'cause I close early on Wednesdays. It was just me, and Buddha was outside watching the door. I wanted to have a one-on-one and didn't really want people to see her comin' or goin'.

"How you doin', Mira?" I walked around the desk and hugged her.

In spite of our predicaments, we were still cool with each other. And we checked on each otha here and there. I don't know, maybe seeing who would die first.

She took a seat on the leather couch against the side wall of my office. "You want somethin' to drink or you alright?"

"You already know what I like, if you got it," she responded.

I walked over to the minibar and fixed up a Remi and cranberry for her and straight Remi for me. I took a seat next to her.

"What's new with you, Mira?" I made small talk.

"Same ol'. A bitch just tryin' to keep her head above water and get a few extra years outta life." She sipped her drink. "So far, so good. I don't have full blown AIDS yet, so I guess I'm blessed on that end. What about you, Rou?" she asked with raised eyebrows.

"I feel just like you feel. How shit lookin' over at the 'Lexx'?"

"I don't know. I haven't been fuckin' 'round in there lately. I been dancin' in the cracka clubs, Gold Rush and Tootsies."

"When you switched over?" I inquired.

"'Bout two months ago, right after customs hit the docks for those five thousand keys, since them cats been crabbin' with that cash in the club. You know how it go. A drought hit the streets, a drought hit the stip clubs – black ones that is. So I been fuckin' 'round in the white club gettin' that year-round, never-have-a-drought, legit, baby-I-spent-the-bill-money money," she joked. "Plus, you know it's ten and twenty in' there instead of five and ten," she said, referring to the ten-dollar tabletop and twenty-dollar lap dances in the white clubs compared to the five-dollar tabletop and ten-dollar lap dances in the black clubs.

"By the way, word on the street is you got robbed couple months ago or somethin'. That's true?" She watched me.

My jaws tightened, "Yeah, some niggas hit me up. They got me good, used hoes and all to set me up."

"Women are the root of all evil," she smirked. "They'll get you killed, robbed, strung out, or broke. Since when you started slippin' like that, bruh? You got more game than most cats. And especially with the money you pay those niggas to watch your back. Shit, that fool outside had me spread eagle on the wall like the police or somethin'."

"You right. But I fault myself as much as I fault them. After all, it was me who gave the order to let the broads through. But that's the past. I found out who it was, so..."

"You did? Who was it? Somebody you know, huh?"

"Yeah, somebody I know real good. Actually, that's why I needed to holla at you." I eased into the reason for the meeting.

"Um hm, so what? You planning get-back. I knew it was some kind of reason you called me here. So what you need, bruh? What, you need me to set 'em up for you? They used bitches so it's only right if you use a bitch in return, right?"

"Right, but you might not like what I have in mind about settin' 'em up."

"Bruh, you know ain't no shame in my game. If I gotta fuck, suck, whatever. I know you gonna break bread. Plus, I might can make them come up off some chips, too, before shit hit the fan." She sipped her drink.

"That's exactly what I need you to do. Fuck and suck. I want you to give that nigga that shit."

She spit her drink out, "What?"

"I said I want you to give one of them niggas this slow death we carryin' 'round," I stated seriously.

"Rouseau, have you lost your damn mind?! You know exactly how I feel about that shit. No matter how mad I am at the world, I can't blame nobody but myself. When I, or *we*, first found out about this shit, that was my exact attitude. I told myself that it was going to be a lot of dead men walking. 'Cause I was gonna scar as many niggas as possible. But, as I got past the initial shock, I promised myself that I wouldn't use my anger to start killing people. Maybe take niggas for whatever I can, but not kill 'em that way. Rou, that shit ain't right. I can't deal with somethin' like that on my conscience. I still strip. I still fuck for money. But I do it safely. Since we found out we were sick, I know for a fact that I haven't passed this disease off to nobody."

"I'm not asking you to do it out of anger. I'm asking you to do it for money."

"There's no amount of money that can make me do that shit." She turned away from me.

"I'll pay you a hundred thousand dollars to give one nigga the devil's disease."

Her body stiffened. She jerked her head back towards me and eyed me for a long time without sayin' shit. Yeeaah, I know what she was thinking. "A hundred stacks buys a lot of medicine."

"One hundred thousand dollars? You're serious, huh?" she paused and shook her head. "Man, Rouseau, I don't know about this. This shit just sound too crazy."

I knew I had her on the ropes, so I threw out my ace of spades.

"Just because they robbed me isn't the only reason I wanna scar this nigga. It's really about a whole 'nother issue."

I dropped my head.

"What? What's the other reason, Rou?"

When I lifted my head, my eyes held tears.

"Dis nigga, Chill, was, or *is*, one of Tank's best friends," I lied. "I heard that they are cousins."

I knew Tank was still a sore spot for her.

Her eyes narrowed, and she put on a unit, "Are you serious?"

Time for the body blow.

I turned and looked her directly in the eye and lifted her chin, "Mira, Tank stole somethin' precious from us – my girl and your sister. Then he took the most precious thing of all – our lives." I paused for effect. "This is not just about my gamblin' house gettin' robbed. Nah… It's about us gettin' robbed of our lives. It's about honoring your sister's memory. It's about tryin' to get a little bit of payback and a step closer to closure. We can't catch up with that cat, Tank, so we have to do the next best thing."

She was shedding silent tears.

"That's right, Mira. He took one of ours so we take one of his." I leaned over and hugged her tight as she cried.

"I need you with me on this one, Mira. Your sister needs you," I whispered. "Are you down for us, Mira? Are you down for yourself?"

Silence.

She took a dep breath, closed her eyes, and reopened them. "I'll do it. I'll do it for me, you, and my sister."

I gave her a few minutes to compose herself, and then I laid the plan out from start to finish. I had gotten Chill's number out of Shay's phone one night. Now it was time to put it to use.

CHAPTER 28

"A nigga done come a long way," I thought to myself, as I whipped to 'da Leaf,' watchin' da scenery as I passed by. Crackas might call it "nostalgia", a word I borrowed from Chill. But I call it "thinkin' about what da fuck not to go back to". I'm a young millionaire. They tried to tell me dat money was the root of all evil. They got it backwards. *Not* having money is da root of all evil! 'Cause dat's when a muhfucka do any and everything to get it.

I went from sellin' for a nigga, gettin' twenty-five off of every hundred, to now, cookin', choppin', and baggin' up sac for da whole week. We cook up 5 chickens each week, for dimes (ten dollars), quarters (twenty-five dollars) eightballs (three and a half grams), half a zinc (fourteen grams), and zincs (twenty-eight grams). All hard. I sell jugglers. See, a nigga like me was taught to go for the quick flip. While anotha nigga sittin' ova there tryin' to stretch dat shit out, I'm putting out shit dat a hustla or baser can double dey money or smoke. Shit… both. You cut twenty dollars out my dimes, forty, forty-five out of my quarters. Plus, my eightballs go for eighty dollars, instead of a hundred like da competition, wit' da four grams instead of three and a half.

I make twenty-five to forty stacks out of a three shift day, on a regular basis. I make damn near double dat on weekends, first and fifteenth, and holidays. Like I say, my life ain't always been dis lovely, but it is now. It's been a long, hard journey, and I gotta lot of grief to give a muhfucka who think money done made a nigga soft. I do kill babies and baby mommas. Nigga, everybody can get it. It's a long, slow road to hell, and I'm da fire and brimstone.

Thing is I 'on't think I do dis shit fo' da cash no mo'. I do it for da thrill, 'cause it's all I know. I wouldn't make it a regular world, but I'm da king in my world. Da world of guns, dope, money, and hoes.

Da American Dream! Ha!

I scope out da scene as I pull in da lot. Shit is dead. I see my mornin' shift workers out and about. Chaunce and Goon should be here at nine. I always get here early just to organize. I get out my car and head upstairs to da honeycomb to get situated.

Damn! Two bad ass hoes. I ain't never seen dem 'round here. Instantly suspicious.

"What dey do, ladies?" I call out as they headed in my direction. Must be headed to da stairs. "Where y'all goin'? Can I go?"

They smiled. "We just came from our cousin Trell apartment, Mr. Nosy," one of 'em said.

"Oh, dat's my homegirl," talkin' 'bout a girl who stayed in one of da 'partments down da hall. Dat explains it. Guard's down.

"Just your homegirl, huh?" One of 'em asked sarcastically.

"Oh, nah... I ain't neva fuck. We just cool," I lied.

"So what you doin' up dis early?" they asked.

"Early bird gets da worm," I said as I stuck da key in da bargate lock and pulled da door open. "So which one of you can I have? Or can I have both?" I joked, as they stopped in front of me. I unlocked da reinforced metal door, which was painted over to look like wood.

"Both of us?" da otha one said lookin' me up and down. "I don't think you can handle one of us."

"We won't know 'til we try. How 'bout y'all shoot dem name and numbers, and I'll holla lata and we can make some shit happen." I stepped across da threshold and turned around.

"Yeah, that sounds cool," she said diggin' in her purse. "But I don't accept collect calls."

"What?" I asked confused.

She pulled out her fire and her homegirl did da same.

"ATF," dey both screamed, "Lay down on da ground!"

Next thing I know, all type of agents comin' out da woodwork. Shoved me on da ground hard.

Fuck!

"What da fuck y'all cracaks doin? Y'all ain't got no warrant," I growled. One of da crackas shoved a piece of paper under my nose.

"Read it and pray," a big muhfucka wit' shades and a crewcut told me.

They cuffed me and search me. Then they proceeded to tear da whole apartment up. I already knew they wasn't gonna find shit. I hadn't been by Quanda crib to pick up my cookin' utensils. And da ten birds I dropped off last night were stashed in da wall. You'd have to be a carpenter to get to 'em. Or you had to know 'bout 'em and where to look.

"Where's it at, M1?" an agent kneeled down in front of me.

"Fuck y'all crackas," I said calmly. "You know a person could get killed for disrespectin' people da way y'all do. But since I'm a law-abiding citizen, I'll let my lawyers handle it."

"Threatening a federal agent, are we?" he smirked.

I raised my head up, "I don't make threats or promises. I make shit happen." I was arrogant and cocky.

Until I heard one of 'em say, . "It's inside the wall. Gimme the tools. Intel said inside the hallway closet wall."

How da fuck? Intel?

Now I got butterflies in my stomach like I was on a roller coaster.

It's only four people who know 'bout dat spot and one of 'em been erased off da map.. so dat leave me, Chaunce, and Goon.

Who snitched?

"We got it!" anotha cracka cried out.

"Jackpot!" anotha yelled.

My heart was in my ass.

"Hey, Mitch, we got ten of 'em."

"Shit, Thomas! This has got to be eighty-five percent pure. Look like that pink panther shit." Eighty-five was da purest form of coke on da streets.

"Yeah, Rick... Pink, pearly and looks like glass."

"Alright, alright, you two. David, Mike, pick 'em up and get 'em out of here. Dana, Marie, start the paperwork," he commanded.

"Why do we have to do the paperwork, Mitch?" Dana whined.

"'Cause I'm in charge. Now get started."

"You hear that, Mr. M1? Doesn't look like you'll be making any plans for later tonight, sweetie," Marie taunted.

"Besides, we don't do drug dealers," Dana said and laughed.

"Fuck you. I don't do shiteaters!" I shot back, "And I'm ready to holla at my lawyers so save all dat rap about workin' deals and shit. Real niggas don't fold," I yelled as they escorted me out da door.

When they got me outside and put me in da back of one of their vehicles, I saw dat da projects had come alive. I also saw Goon and Chaunce standin' in da crowd watchin' everything. We made contact wit' our eyes. I was watchin' their body language and reaction to see which one – or did both of 'em tell somethin'. I need to holla at Chill. If they tellin', then they probably won't contact him. I'll have to make my lawyers do it.

––––––

Chill, 8:50 a.m.

"Yeah," I answered, as I rolled over and picked my cell phone up off the nightstand.

"Hey, fool, dey got M1!" a loud, excited voice yelled in the phone. "Dey got 'em in da car right now!"

"Who is dis? Who got M1?" I asked, confused and groggy.

"Dis Chaunce, my nigga! ATF got M1! He sittin' in da car right now!" he exclaimed.

I sat up, "Hold up, hold up. Calm down, fool." My head was instantly cleared by a shot of adrenaline. "Did dey snatch anything?"

"I didn't s – oh, shit!" he shot out excitedly.

"What?" I got butterflies in my stomach.

"Dey bringin' down guns and carrying some bags and shit."

"Wait. Don't even rap no mo'," I stopped him. "Meet me at McDonald's on 150th Street and 7th Avenue. We'll talk then. Right now I'm finna call our lawyers. I'll holla."

I hung up and called our attorneys.

"Blakely, Thomas & Associates," the receptionist answered.

"Hey, how you doin', Lucinda? It's Mante'."

"Hey, Mante'. I'm fine, and yourself?" She responded cheerfully. "Is everything okay?" she questioned.

"Unfortunately not," I answered. "Is Leanne or Shelley available?"

"Well, Shelley's in court, but Leanne's here. Hold on, I'll tell her you're on the line."

"Thank you. Tell her it's urgent."

I had slipped on clothes and was headed out the door without even brushing my grill.

"Are you okay?" Leanne asked, as soon as she was on the phone.

That's why Shelley and her were loved by clients and hated by other attorneys. Because they genuinely cared about their clients, worked hard, and didn't give you any bullshit. They always did what was absolutely best for their clients.

"I'm okay, but M1 – my bad – I mean Mario just got picked up by the ATF."

"Are you on your cell phone?" she asked.

"Yeah. Why?"

"Alright, just come to the office. We'll talk when you get here."

"Alright, but I gotta meet up with my homeboys. They were on the scene."

"Well, bring them along with you. I want to talk to them. And stay off your cell phone."

"I feel you."

"How soon will you be here?" she asked.

"Gimme about an hour."

"Cool," she said, and hung up.

All three of us got to the law firm. It was situated in Miami Lakes, in an upscale neighborhood, but off the normal path for law firms. They had taken a ten-bedroom villa-style home and made it into an office. They were the only firm in that area. But it didn't matter because their clients all spoke highly of them. Those who needed to know, or could afford to know, knew just where they were located.

We all got situated in Leanne's office. Shelley was also there, back from court. Shelley had blond hair and was from Florida, and Leanne had dark brown hair and was from Minnesota. But they both had one thing in common: They both looked like they belonged on international runways, modeling beside the world's top models. But that's a facade that a lot of prosecutors fell for when they first started out ten years ago. That perception got a lot of prosecutors burned for underestimating them. Now the word was out all through the State of Florida that these were the most brilliant and hardest working attorneys around, perhaps even in the nation. They weren't underestimated in the courtroom any longer.

They were feared.

Leanne stated, "I made some calls, and he hasn't been fully processed yet. After we finish up here, Shelley and I are gonna head to the federal detention center. But I was able to reach one of my contacts through back channels. Apparently ten kilos of cocaine were found, along with four guns. One Mac 11, an AK-47, and two nine millimeter handguns." She paused and watched Chaunce and Goon.

I simply shook my head.

Shelley took over. "What we need from you two is everything that you know. We need to know what you saw today and everything you know about that apartment."

Chaunce and Goon looked over at me for approval.

I nodded my head.

They both began relaying everything they knew and saw. The attorneys recorded everything so there wouldn't be any misinterpretations. When they were done, Leanne jumped on the phone, and Shelley began to speak.

"We're going to head down there now and see what else we can find out. Plus, talk to him and get his side. We'll have to set up a hearing for bonds. Although, I can say, unless we find a sensible judge, his bond is going to be sky-high or none at all. Hope for the best, expect the worst." She didn't sugarcoat anything. She looked directly at me. "We'll be in touch, Mante', as soon as we leave him. As usual, you know we'll do everything in our considerable power to minimize and, ultimately, neutralize this situation and whatever repercussions that could stem from it. So just be patient and let us work," she ended.

With that said, she stood, shook our hands, and we left. One thing we didn't have to worry about was attorney fees. M1 had two hundred and fifty thousand on retainer that they kept in a trust fund and drew out whatever fees were needed. Me, I had the same amount in retainer fees that they were holding. Knock on wood – hopefully, I'd never need it.

Chaunce and Goon followed me in their own whip. So they peeled off. Before they left, I told 'em to stay from 'round the Leaf for a few days and that I'd give them any message M1 had to pass on.

———

M1
12:14 P.M.

"Somebody wants to see you, kingpin," one of the marshalls said sarcastically.

"I 'on't know shit! So tell 'em don't waste dey time tryin'," I shot back.

"You turnin' down your attorney visit?" he asked with a half-ass grin.

I frowned, "Attorney?" I ain't even used da pipe yet. "Hell, nah... I ain't turnin' shit down!

I stood up, let him cuff me, and followed him to da attorney room. "How my lawyer know I'm here?" I asked to myself.

"Maybe one of your druglord friends told him," he said and laughed.

We reached da room, and he opened da door. When I saw Leanne and Shelley, I was happier than a punk in a garden full of dicks.

The marshall told them he'd be right outside and closed da door.

"Damn, y'all are definitely a sight for sore eyes," I acknowledged. "How y'all knew I got jammed up?" I questioned.

"Mante' informed us. Are you okay?" Leanne asked.

"Hell nah! I ain't okay. How Chill know I'm here?"

"Your friends Chauncy and Goon called him when you were put inside one of the ATF vehicles," Shelley answered.

"Those slimy muhfuckas! When I get out, I'm a kill dey whole family tree."

They both looked at me, confused.

"Dey da reason I'm here right now. One or both of dem is a snitch."

"It's possible, but are you sure?. They seemed too concerned and responded too quickly to the situation," Shelley stated.

"Besides," Leanne pulled some papers out of her briefcase, "We already thought of that. We did a quick, but thorough, inquiry into their background. We actually checked that angle. I called in some favors to get it done quick. They don't have any cases pending, and their names are not on any informant lists." She slid the papers over.

"How reliable is this stuff?" I asked, confused.

"Like I said, quick, but highly accurate," she answered.

Shelley added, "They even offered to pay us, before they knew it was handled."

"It has to be some kind of mistake. They are the only ones who knew the interior of that apartment. Them and one more person."

"Well, what about that person? Gimme the name and we'll check them out," Shelley asked, pen ready.

"Don't waste your time. They couldn't tell," I responded, as my mind flipped through information.

"Why?" Leanne asked.

I looked her in the eyes, "Because they're no longer among the living."

They both watched me for a minute.

"Well, either way, we'll find out for sure. It'll come out in the discovery, but I have some other contacts researching for us in the meantime. Trust me, if anything, and I mean *anything*, is there, *whoever* it is, we'll find out," Leanne assured.

"What about bond or somethin', anything? I don't care how much it costs. I need to be free. I got some people that need extended vacations," I explained cooly.

"You let us worry about the bond and the case – period. We don't need you interfering and, as you say, putting anyone on extended vacations. Anything that can, legally, be done to help you will be done, I assure you. So that, in the end, that will be more than sufficient." She eyed me directly. "You know how we operate. You paid for the hardest working lawyers in the world, and that's what you got," Shelley stated firmly.

"Let us work, Mario. Sit back and be patient. Let us work. That's what you paid us for."

I smiled, "Dat's what you told me two years ago, when I had dat block in da whip."

"Yeah, and we got your ass out. So I insist you take our advice again," suggested Leanne.

Shelley pulled out a recorder.

"Explain, and start from the beginning. Don't leave nothing out, even if you feel it's not important."

I ran down da whole shit from start to finish.

Shelley asked when I finished, "So they used man's biggest weakness to pull you in?"

"Yeah, I guess so," I responded honestly, feelin' stupid, 'cause I know I'm a rawer nigga than dat. I slipped.

Leanne picked up on dis, "Don't be too hard on yourself. Everybody makes mistakes. Just chill. We'll handle everything," she assured.

"Anything you need to tell Mante'?" Shelley asked.

"Just tell him to go by Kendra house. She'll tell him what to do."

"Will do. You just take it easy. From what you've told us, it's going to be a fight. But I see a lot of loopholes. We'll research and see what we come up with."

They both stood up, hugged me, and called for da marshall.

CHAPTER 29

"We'll have a bottle of the Chateau Lamondotte Saint Emilion '96," Arthur informed the host.

Him and Lauren were dining at La Fontaine de Trevi, a five-star restaurant, noted for having the best French cuisine outside of France. It was located in Miami Beach. You could see numerous politicians, entertainers, athletes, Cuban and Colombian druglords there on any given night.

"Excellent choice, sir," the maitre d'hotel responded. "I'll be right back with your selection, sir." He bowed and left.

Arthur looked at Lauren, "How was your day, dear? You look frustrated," Arthur said, genuinely concerned.

"I am frustrated. I've been working on the Douglass Industries' accounts all week, which wouldn't be so bad except for the fact that they call everyday, five or six times a day. Some kind of merger deadline they're trying to meet. So they've been harassing me nonstop.

"I'm very sorry to hear that, darling."

"Yeah, at first they wanted everything by Monday, which meant I could've worked on it over the weekend. But now they've pushed it up to Friday."

The maitre d' came back, popped the cork, and poured two glasses of the expensive red wine. "Your waiter will be with you shortly, sir, madame," he bowed.

"Actually, could you have him hold off for ten minutes?" Arthur requested.

"Not a problem, sir. Is there anything else I can do?"

"No, thank you. That's all." He turned and left.

Arthur picked up where they left off.

"Lauren, you should've told me. We could've dined at home. That way you could've been working. I don't mean to waste your time."

"No, that's okay, Arthur. It does me plenty of good to get out and get some fresh air," Lauren admitted.

"If you want, I could send a couple of my company accountants to assist you and your staff," he offered.

"No, thank you." She looked at him pointedly. "My staff is more than capable. It's not the first deadline that I 've had to meet. Nor will it be the last."

"I know. I wasn't insinu –"

"I know. I know. I'm just a little uptight. I apologize."

But it was more than just work that was troubling Lauren.

"No need, dear. I completely understand. You know better than most how I can be a real prick after those crazy work days," he chuckled.

Lauren grinned. "That I do," she admitted.

The waiter came to take their orders.

"Are you ready to order, sir? Madame? Or would you be needing more time?" he inquired.

"No, we're ready, actually. Ah, I'll have the jarret d'agneau with the tian de legumes and, for an appetizer, the escargot a la bourguignonne," he ordered.

"And for you, madame?"

"I'll have the tuna tartare as an appetizer, and, for the entrée, the canard au miel et haricots vert," she ordered.

"Excellent! I'll be back with your appetizers. Is there anything else I can get you?" he asked.

"No, thank you. That's it," Arthur responded.

"Alright. I shall return." He bowed and left.

"You know, this place makes me think of when we went to France last year. You came down with the flu, remember? Instead of spending the week exploring, we spent the whole time the hotel room. Me taking care of you and feeding you." He looked nostalgic.

Yeah, and the whole time I was wishing it was Mante'.

"I never once left your side, except to get you medicine."

"No, you didn't leave me, Arthur," Lauren admitted.

No, you didn't do me how Mante' did me, she thought. Matter of fact, as Lauren sat here and thought of it now, Arthur had been reliable, dependable, and as far as she knew, he had never lied to her.

"Lauren, this has been the most remarkable two years of my entire life. Even when we have spats, I'm just happy to have somebody to have a spat with. I wouldn't trade one of our bad days together for a million good days without you. You give me substance. I don't remember life before you, and I definitely don't want to live it without you. I ask God everyday, "What did I do to deserve my very own angel?".. You don't just have a place in my heart, you are my heartbeat, the very essence of my being."

The waiter appeared out of nowhere, pushing a cart with a silver-covered tray. He stopped at their table.

Arthur stood up.

Lauren's heart started beating fast as Arthur came around to her side of the table and stood before her.

The waiter uncovered the tray, and Lauren gasped. There sat on the tray a ten-carat heart-cut diamond set in platinum.

Arthur dropped on both knees. Everyone in the restaurant was staring.

Arthur took Lauren's hand in his and looked deeply in her eyes, "I think about you, dream about you. I breathe you. Everywhere I go, I see you." Tears slowly slid down Lauren's cheeks. "I adore you. I cherish you. Honey, I worship the ground you walk on." Now, *he* had tears in his eyes. "Honey, I know at times I aggravate you. I know I'm not perfect. But I love you, Lauren – soul, mind and body. Please give me the privilege of spending the rest of my life with you," he pleaded.

Lauren's mind was moving a thousand miles per hour. Deep down inside, she knew that she wasn't in love with Arthur, although she sincerely cared very deeply for him. In the two years they'd been together, there had been way more ups than downs, and they were happy. But her heart belonged to one man – D'Mante' Stevens. But it didn't seem like that was going to happen. She'd been waiting forever for Mante' to come around. Instead, first chance he got, he lied and left her hanging for someone else. There comes a time in a woman's life when she just has to say it wasn't meant to be. For the last month and a half, she'd done a good job of avoiding him, but now, it was time to really move on. Although she didn't love Arthur how he loved her, she knew she'd be good to him. So, she accepted.

"Yes, Arthur, I'll marry you."

Everyone in the restaurant clapped. Arthur looked relieved. He took the ring, slid it on her finger, and kissed her passionately. Lauren continued to cry, but they were not tears of joy. They were tears of regret that things couldn't have been different for her and Mante'.

"I'm sorry, Mante'," she thought.

CHAPTER 30

I feel like shit. I've been throwing up and having dizzy spells. My throat feels like it's swollen. I've been feeling so drained – no energy at all. I *would* catch the flu right before I'm supposed to go to the Bahamas for the weekend. That damn Theraflu has not been doing shit. I've been drinking that stuff back to back. Hopefully the doctor will give me some antibiotics and I'll feel better in the morning.

Randy's going to be so disappointed if I cancel out at the last minute. Of course, I will be, too. I've been fantasizing about getting my toes sucked on Paradise Island all week. The thought gives me goose bumps all over.

"L'Shay Poitier?" Debra, the receptionist, called out, bringing me out of my fantasy.

"Right here, Debra," I responded.

"They're ready for you."

I walked through the frosted glass door that separated the waiting area from the exam area into one of the examination rooms. A nurse came in shortly after and measured my weight, temperature, and blood pressure. She then had me change into a gown.

Ten minutes later, the doctor arrived.

"Hi, Shay. How's the family?" Doctor Mitchell asked.

"Oh, everyone is fine. How 'bout you and yours?"

"The same. The same. Need a vacation. Brenda's been nagging forever. Figure I better give in before she whines me into an early grave," he joked about his wife.

I smiled.

"So what's troubling you, Shay? I've read your chart and complaints. But I want to hear it from you verbatim."

I told him all of my symptoms.

"I'm going to order some bloodwork, and I'll need some urine samples. So you'll have to urinate in the cup for me." He felt up under my chin where it met my neck. "Your lymph nodes are swollen. So your body is fighting some type of infection. The bloodwork will tell us. Then I can put you on some antibiotics. Probably just a summer flu. Just use the cup. Put it in that slot, and the nurse will be right in to do your bloodwork."

Forty-five minutes later

"Shay, the tests show that your white blood cell count is extremely high, as is normal when they're fighting infections, but I don't see any type of flu virus or similar viral strain. I am seeing other things that I need to check. Now, don't take this the wrong way. I know you're married."

I immediately squinted my face up and my heart rate accelerated.

"Your chart says that the last time you took an HIV test was five months ago."

"What are you saying, Doctor Mitchell? You think I have AIDS?" I questioned nervously. If Jap gave me something, I'll kill his ass.

"No, I just want to test you to be sure. As I said, I see some other things going on in your blood and would like to check all possibilities. I know you and know your family, but I know the consequences of a cheating husband. We have a twenty-minute test kit. So you don't have to wait the usual two or three weeks."

"No problem. Do whatever you need to do. But I'm sure it's some type of flu or cold." I mustered up false bravado.

"And I also had Nurse Davis give you a pregnancy test. Based on the symptoms I'm seeing, that could be something else to look for. I know you're on the pill, but have you been taking them?" he inquired.

"I uh… well, I… I mean I haven't taken them in a couple of months. But I haven't had any unprotected sex. I mean 'cause Jap and I are separated," I sputtered.

He looked at me thoughtfully and said, "I see."

"But, I mean, do whatever you think is necessary, Dr. Mitchell."

Thirty minutes later

Dr. Mitchell's face held a grim looking expression as he re-entered the exam room. I immediately began to fear the worst. I sat on the edge of the examination table. He sat in a chair that was in front of a counter, on which sat Q-tips, cotton balls, those Popsicle sticks they put in your mouth and other doctor's office accessories.

He began, "Shay, I've known you for a long time, practically watched you grow up. You know I treat a lot of your family." I sat stiff and held my breath. "That's why it saddens me to have to sit here and tell you that our tests show two things," he paused and took his glasses off.

I closed my eyes and took a deep breath.

Please, God! Oh, please spare me, Lord! Please don't do me like this!

The tears flowed down my face.

He continued with watery eyes, "Shay, the tests show that you've contracted HIV, the virus that causes AIDS, and also that you're pregnant. You g –"

"NO, NO!. PLEASE TELL ME THERE'S BEEN SOME MISTAKE! IT'S GOT TO BE! HELP ME! PLEASE, PLEASE!. I DON'T WANT TO DIE!" I cried and shook uncontrollably. "WHAT ABOUT MY SON?" I sobbed. "AHHHH! WHAT ABOUT MY BABY?"

Dr. Mitchell stood up and hugged me tight. I clawed his shirt with both hands and sobbed into his chest.

I suddenly thought about Jap.

"No, noooo! OH, GOD, WHAT HAVE I DONE?" I shouted out. "WHY, WHY?" I leaned back, looked into Dr. Mitchell's eyes, and then everything went blank

———

M1, 10:30 A.M.

"Your Honor, Mr. Woods has numerous positive ties to the city. He is part-owner of a construction firm, which not only builds churches and youth centers to further education for kids, but he does so through his own not-for-profit organization at no cost to the congregations or taxpayers. He oversees and coaches Little League football and basketball teams. In addition, he sponsors trips for underprivileged youths to different places around the country," Leanne informed Judge Matthews. "I as –"

The prosecutor cut her off. "That would be all fine and well, Your Honor, if he didn't do it with the proceeds from drugs," he stated sarcastically.

"Your Honor, the State is making accusations and assumptions, at best. My client is innocent of the charges against him. Furthermore, he has not been charged with a capital offense, and, as stated by the laws of this country, is entitled to a reasonable bond." She looked behind her. "We have Reverend Bruce from the New Birth Ministries and Bishop Wright from St. Jude and the World here on my client's behalf. We also have Rose Mitchell, director of the Heart of the City Youth and Rec-Centers, which have eight centers in Miami. In addition, we have Felicia Rodriguez, director of Second Chance Youth Outrreach, as well as thirty friends and relatives," she finished up. "Mr. Woods is not only well liked, but he is beloved by family, friends, and his community alike. At this time, I ask that Your Honor grant Mr. Woods not only a bond, but the reasonable bond that he is entitled to."

Yeah, she broke it down for me. This fat-ass cracker need to go on 'head and gimme my bond so I can get out dis shit. Lookin' in da crowd, I see Chill did his thang fillin' up da courtroom. I wonder how much he paid all these people to be here for me. Dat's my nigga.

Da judge looked over da paperwork while he considered.

Dat's when da government spoke.

"Your Honor, before you consider, we ask that you take into account that Mr. Woods is also a suspect in a current attempted murder case." He paused as Leanne and him glared at each other. "And you know, as well as my colleague, Ms. Blakely, that attempted murder is a life felony and not entitled to any such bond." He looked smug.

I felt like somebody hit me in da stomach wit' a sledge hammer.

"Your Honor, this is preposterous!. We have no information on these charges. Mr. Collins is trying to make up charges to keep my client further incarcerated. He's trying to impede justice by using blackball tactics, Your Honor. This is ridiculous!" my lawyer defended.

"Judge, we were just informed of the matter this morning. I haven't had a proper chance to look into it. This is not any type of delay tactic. We have no control over when crimes come to light."

"Your Ho –"

The judge cut her off. "I'm going to assess no bond for now, until we straighten this matter out."

I ignored da rest. Welcome to da FED.

Dese bitches play dirty!

———

SHAY

When I came to, I was in a room that looked like a hospital room, but a little smaller. Ten minutes later, a nurse came in.

"Oh, hi, darling. You're awake." She walked over to me.

"Where am I?" My throat was dry as desert sand.

"You're still Dr. Mitchell's office. This is just one of the special rooms we keep for emergencies," she informed. "You passed out about two hours ago." She handed me a glass of water.

"I'll let him know you're awake now. Just take it easy, okay?" She left the room.

He came in a few minutes later.

"How are you feeling, Shay?" he asked, full of concern.

Seeing his face brought back all the pain and hurt.

"I dont' know what to do. I don't know how to go on."

"I know you may not believe this, but everything is going to be fine. I know your family will stick by you, and so will I. You'll have plenty of support. Most of all, you have God. Pray, my dear. Pray."

"If God cared, then he wouldn't have given me this disease."

"Dear child, we must not blame God for choices that we are free to make."

I began to cry while Dr. Mitchell held my hand.

"Shay, there is someone waiting outside that I want you to meet. Her name is Michelle Powell. She's a counselor and therapist. She's going to talk to you and explain some things you probably didn't know. She'll help you to understand, Shay. Just listen to her."

He went and opened the door, and a short, thin, middle-aged woman came in. She wore her hair in a bun. She was wearing black slacks with a pink top.

She walked over to my bed.

"Hi, Shay. I'm Michelle. Doctor Mitchell asked me to speak with you and explain some things to you about the disease you carry."

"What's there to explain?" I felt so drained. "My life is over!"

"Actually, that's the first thing to understand," Michelle began. "Your life is not over. If you take care of yourself and take the proper medication, you can still live and die old. This isn't the eighties when no one understood this disease. There've been numerous medial advancements in regards to treatment. Although there's no cure, you can live comfortably enough with HIV. But you've got to believe. And, most of all, you can't give up."

I heard her voice, but I wasn't listening. I was thinking about how and when. I used condoms every time I had sex. I've never had unprotected sex except one time that kept coming back to me. One of the last times I was with Rouseau, on the fourth of July. I remember it feeling like he had no condom on. I remember how drunk I was and how good it felt. But what I remember most is being so caught up in the moment that I didn't stop him. I didn't want to stop.

I remember his cum dripping out of me the next day.

Now I realize, that for those few minutes that I thought felt so good and so intense, I've given up my life.

I chose death.

"Shay. Shay, are you listening?" Dr. Mitchell's voice brought me out of my thoughts.

"I'm... I'm sorry."

"I already told Michelle that you're married. Did it...uh...did you..." He was uncomfortable. Is your husband the cause of this?"

I knew what he was asking.

"No, I'm the cause of this. And, yes, I've been with others besides my husband." I stopped and looked up at them. Doc' looked taken back, and Michelle showed no emotion. "Me and Jap are separated. I...I haven't had sex with him in over two months."

Michelle inquired, "Were these others unprotected?"

"No...I mean yes... It wasn't supposed to be." I began crying once again. "I...was...drunk!"

She stroked my hair and held my hand. "Shay, I know how much this hurts. I know how angry, confused, and sad you are right now. But I need you to be strong, dear child. Be strong." She kissed my forehead.

"I need to know, Shay. Did this incident happen before or after you discontinued sex with your husband?" my doctor asked.

I was quiet for few seconds, "After. It was after," I answered.

"Are you certain?" he questioned.

I silently nodded my head.

"We still have to get him tested. Just to be certain," he informed me.

I was so confused. Thinking what if it happened earlier and I didn't know. My heart raced, "Please let Jap be okay," I pleaded through tears. "He has to be okay to take care of our son."

"He will be, Shay. He will be," they both responded to my pleas.

"Now, Shay, you have to tell us," Dr. Mitchell began, "who was it, Shay? Who gave you HIV?"

CHAPTER 31

CHILL
FRIDAY, AUGUST 21, 3:30 P.M.

"Hello. Can I speak to Chill?" a woman's voice asked.

"Dis Chill. Who dis?" I asked, trying to catch the voice. I did not miss the fact that she called out my nickname and called me on my private cell phone, for friends and family.

So it had to be somebody I knew on a personal level.

"This is Deborah," she answered.

I got quiet as I tried to remember who the hell Deborah was.

She started laughing.

"What's so funny?" I asked, still wondering.

She answered, "You."

"Why you say that?"

"'Cause you sittin' there trying to figure out who I am. Boy, stop racking your brain, 'cause you don't even know me."

Now I was really confused.

"Well, in that case, how you got this number?"

"I know, I know. Shay already told me that this was your personal phone. She said you might get mad at her for giving it to me. But please, don't be upset, sweetie. I really, really wanted to meet you."

Shay gave her my number?

"Nah, I ain't hot wit' you, l'il momma. What dey do?"

"I don't know, Mr. Chill. I made the first move. Ball is in your court now," she said, full of sass.

I smirked, "You don't beat around da bush, huh? I'm sayin', what made you wanna meet me?"

"Shay always talking 'bout Jap friend this and Jap friend that. She act like she can't stand you. But Trenice did say you was sexy."

"Trenice said I was sexy?"

"Don't let it go to your head. But you know how women talk. So, I got curious. Then Shay finally showed me a picture with you and Jap. And I have to agree with Trenice. You *are* sexy, boy."

"Well, then we need to even this out. 'Cause right now, you got the advantage. I mean, having seen me and all. So now I need to see what you workin' wit'. You might be a boogar."

"Uh-uh, baby. Let me stop you right there. I'm not trying to be conceited or nothin', but I promise you I'm top notch. What y'all niggas call 'dime'."

"Damn, it's like dat." Shay did have some fine homegirls, including Trenice. "What's up wit' tonight then?" I asked.

"What about it?"

"Why don't you stop by da crib around nine and we'll get to know one another."

"How about I meet you at your house around nine, and we go out, eat. Then we can come back to your house and, as you say, get to know one another."

I laughed, "I'm wit' dat, sweetie."

"Why you laughing? A female knows if she's gonna fuck a dude when she first meets him. I told you I'm diggin' you. Plus, I told you I'm curious. What did you think I was curious about? I'm not scaring you by being straight up, am I? I know it makes some men nervous."

"Nah...I respect ya mind. I wouldn't have it any other way. Well, just hit me about seven thirty or eight and I'll give you directions."

"You're not going to duck and dodge my call, are you?"

"L'il momma, I'm a raw nigga, not a flaw nigga," I assured.

"Hmm, that's what your mouth say, but we'll see. By the way, what's your favorite color?"

"Blue. Why?"

"It's a surprise. See you later...Chill."

"I'll holla," I said, and hung up.

———

www.ingramcontent.com/pod-product-compliance
Lightning Source LLC
Chambersburg PA
CBHW060745180626
46818CB00002B/450